"You can go into my bedroom if you'd like."

Instantly he realized he'd made the offer sound suggestive. A Freudian slip if he'd ever had one.

Kelli did a half-snort laugh and retreated into the room. It could have been his imagination but it looked as if her cheeks had reddened. Then again, he could have been mistaken.

Mark stretched out his legs and realized just how tired he felt. Resting his head back on the cushions, he crossed his arms over his chest and closed his eyes. When Kelli was finished he'd offer her some coffee and make a very strong one for himself.

His thoughts went from coffee to the woman who had suddenly become a part of his life. Would she still be after they'd somehow found the justice they both wanted and so desperately needed?

And, more important, how would he feel about it?

Full Force Fatherhood

TYLER ANNE SNELL

First Published in Great Britain 2016
By Mills & Boon, an imprint of HarperCollins*Publishers*
1 London Bridge Street, London, SE1 9GF

Large Print edition 2016

© 2016 Tyler Anne Snell

ISBN: 978-0-263-06656-2

Our policy is to use papers that are natural, renewable and recyclable products and made from wood grown in sustainable forests. The logging and manufacturing processes conform to the legal environmental regulations of the country of origin.

Printed and bound in Great Britain
by CPI Antony Rowe, Chippenham, Wiltshire

Tyler Anne Snell genuinely loves all genres of the written word. However, she's realized that she loves books filled with sexual tension and mysteries a little more than the rest. Her stories have a good dose of both. Tyler lives in Florida with her same-named husband and their mini "lions." When she isn't reading or writing, she's playing video games and working on her blog, *Almost There*. To follow her shenanigans, visit tylerannesnell.com.

This book is for Lillian Grace and Katie.

Lily, thank you for being the coolest kiddo I know. One day you'll be able to appreciate there's a book dedicated to you. Until then I'm sure your mom will hide this sucker until you're older!

Katie, thank you for being a sister, a true friend, and giving me motherhood goals to aspire toward. Not to mention showing me such a strong bond between mother and daughter that it was almost easy to translate it to paper. I'll always love every bit of you and your family!

Chapter One

"Something's not right."

Kelli Crane looked at her husband and sighed. "Making fun of me isn't going to win you any points, Victor," she warned. "Don't poke the bear."

"Because she might poke back?"

He walked into the cabin's bedroom, where she had been lounging with a book, and took a seat at the edge of the bed. In his late thirties, Victor Crane had managed to hold on to his boyish grin with ease. Tall, almost lanky, he had short strawberry blond hair that looked like extensions of the sunlight that fell through the windows, and eyes that mimicked the blue of the sky. She could claim the same kind of brightness about herself, but slightly different—dirty-blond hair, green-gray eyes, a tan that could only be described as sun-kissed—but sometimes when she looked at Victor, her own beauty felt diminished. Staring at her husband of a year and a half, she wondered what their children might look like.

"If you keep mocking me about wanting to keep you safe," she said, "poking back is the first thing I'll do."

Victor held his hands up in defense. "Whatever you say, my love."

She put down her book and smiled. She knew he had only indulged her paranoia by hiring the bodyguard two rooms away. For the past two weeks, he had tried to put her worries to rest. In his line of work as an investigative journalist, sometimes the crazies came out. That didn't mean they should run for help after receiving a few deep-breathing phone calls at the house. However, Kelli couldn't stop her anxiety from mounting as more than just a few calls had come in.

"How's the story coming along?" she asked, setting the book against her stomach. Her hand hovered there a second before she let it drop. "Please tell me you're almost done."

"The *news article* is nearly finished, yes. I should be done by tomorrow." He stood and stretched. "Then we can resume our normal lives."

"You wouldn't want to stay a few more days?" Kelli looked out the window. Victor's family cabin was a few skips away from a crystal-blue lake that looked like a painting, with a pier that Victor had probably walked down since he was a child. Her family had never had moments like that. Then again, if her parents had been alive, she was sure they would have tried. They had been good, loving parents before the car crash had happened when she was younger.

"If this was a vacation, then I'd say yes, but..."

"But you're here to work," she interrupted.

He nodded. "And when that work is done, I have to move on to the next assignment."

"One that I hope won't make me feel we need to hire another bodyguard."

Victor laughed. "Let's be honest. The only reason you hired him was for a little eye candy," he whispered. He raised his eyebrows suggestively, joking with her. Kelli swatted at him.

"Dark hair and muscles galore?" she said. "Who would want that?"

Victor came to her side and bent low. He brushed his lips across hers for a soft kiss.

"Not you," he replied, laughter behind each word.

Kelli smiled. It had been a while since they had been able to spend more than an hour or two a day together. Since they had been married, Victor's assignments had taken him away from their home in Dallas.

But that was going to change soon.

It had to.

"Well, back to the grind. Do you need anything?"

Kelli pictured the ice cream in the freezer but decided against it.

"I think I might take a nap. I still don't feel all that great."

Victor gave her forehead another quick kiss. "Nap away, my love."

And then he was gone.

MARK TRANTON HAD watched the sun set as he finished his routine perimeter check. He might have had a history of traveling internationally and domestically, but this was the first client to bring him to a lakefront property. If he ever took his vacation time, he might consider coming back to a place like this.

In the dwindling light, the isolation felt serene.

He was almost glad that his boss, Nikki Waters, had more or less forced him to take on the weeklong contract with Victor. Even if both Nikki and Victor had said his presence was more for Mrs. Crane's peace of mind.

Since the Orion Security Group was in the middle of an expansion—thanks to a large contract completed two months before by Mark's good friend Oliver—the small company's caseload had tripled. Even though the closest contract start date was two months away. Including one for which Mark would be traveling to Washington for a three-week commitment.

Which was why Nikki had said accompanying the Cranes to a family vacation home in North Carolina was "the closest to a vacation" that Mark would take.

He couldn't complain.

They were on day three of the contract, and Victor and his wife had been nothing but pleasant.

"Are we in the clear?" Victor asked him.

Mr. Crane was standing in the kitchen, beer in hand, when Mark came back inside and locked the door. There was a lightness to his tone but no disrespect. He might not have shared his wife's fear for safety, but he didn't discount Mark's job. Mark respected him more for that.

"I think we'd hear or see someone coming a mile away," Mark answered honestly.

"This place is kind of off the beaten path, but that's why I thought it might do Kelli some good." Victor pulled out another beer from the fridge and started to offer it to Mark but caught himself. He switched out the bottle for water, which Mark thanked him for. Although he could have gotten away with one drink, he wouldn't. A bodyguard needed to stay alert at all times. No exceptions. "Kelli's normally not this anxious. But lately some things have happened that have...well, made her more emotional. I just want to keep her from getting all worked up."

"That's nice of you," Mark said.

"Well, I feel it's the least I can do. I've been working a little more than I should be."

"I can relate to that," Mark said with a quick smile, even though he loved his job. When he wasn't given a new client, he asked for one. He'd been working in the private security business since he was twenty-one. It was as much a part of him as the scars on his back and the muscles he had honed as a job requirement. Pretending that overwork bothered him would be just that.

Pretend.

"You know what I like about you, Mark?"

"Aside from my stoic nature?"

Victor laughed. He seemed always to be laughing.

"Aside from that, I'd have to say I'm surprised you haven't asked me what I'm working on. If I were you, I would have pestered me the last few days."

Mark shrugged. "Once Nikki vets a client, that's pretty much all I need to know. You're a freelance journalist working on a piece for a national news syndicate. I don't need to know the topic to make sure no one shoots you." Victor nodded in assent. "Plus, you said yourself that it wasn't anything that would ruffle anyone's feathers."

"True," he confirmed. "It's a piece spotlighting a private charity foundation based in Texas." It was Victor's turn to shrug. "Nothing too menacing sounding, am I right?"

"Yeah, I'd have to say that—"

The back of the cabin exploded in a fiery ball of glass and wood. The blast sent both men to the ground hard. Heat instantly filled the air, smoke hot on its tail.

Mark was the first to pick himself up, stumbling to his feet, trying to get his bearings. Looking to his right and down the hallway, he couldn't tell what the explosion's origin was. But he knew the outer wall that ran across the office, hallway and master bedroom and bathroom was definitely affected. Flames sprung up everywhere.

Mark went around the counter and hoisted up his client. Through the ringing in his ears, he could hear Victor yell out his wife's name.

The instinct to get the journalist to safety flared within him, but he didn't try to hustle him through the two doors or six windows they had access to. It wouldn't do any good. Victor loved his wife and wouldn't leave her. Mark wouldn't, either.

"Behind me," Mark yelled as he righted the man. Victor's eyes were wide, terrified. He nodded, and they began to move down the hallway as quickly as Mark was comfortable with.

Whatever had blown up had damaged the office opposite the bedroom the most. Through the open door, he could tell the wall was gone. The window in the hallway had blown out, and flames were in the process of devouring the frame. Mark sucked in a breath as he went into the bedroom.

Lying on the floor next to the bed was an unconscious Kelli. Smoke was already hugging the ceiling, billowing out from the bathroom. While Victor bent at his wife's side, Mark ran to see where the new smoke was coming from. The bedroom's outer wall wasn't on fire like the hallway.

He didn't have to look far. Flames were pulsing up the outside of the house, even stretching around to the right side where the guest bedroom was.

That's when Mark saw him.

A figure dressed in black ran around the perimeter of the house, right where Mark had walked minutes earlier.

"Someone's outside," he yelled. Kelli was in Victor's arms, limp. Mark wanted to help her, but he also needed to deal with the person responsible for starting the fire. Victor was about to say something when a horrible crack split the air.

With less than a second to react, Victor threw Kelli forward just as the outer wall crumbled. All Mark could do was watch as Victor was thrown to the ground beneath the wall and part of the roof. With the new source of oxygen, the fire expanded in a violent burst.

Mark went down to his knees, using his body to cover Kelli until everything settled. However, nothing did.

"Save her," yelled Victor. He was trying to move but, in that one horrible moment, both men realized that the weight would be too much for either of them to move. That didn't stop Mark from trying.

He quickly went to the journalist's side and tried with everything he had to lift the largest piece of wall and wood from Victor's back. It didn't budge. Not one bit.

"Save her," Victor yelled again. Another wave of heat rolled through the air. Mark looked around. The escape route into the hallway wasn't going to last much longer.

Mark met the blue eyes of his client, knowing it would be the last time he ever saw them.

"I can save you both," Mark said, though he knew it was a lie. Flames were licking at his back. If they didn't get out now, they wouldn't.

Victor yelled one last plea, making Mark decide the fate of three people all at once.

"She's pregnant!"

Mark didn't hesitate after that. He picked up Kelli and gave Victor one last look.

"I'll come back," he yelled, but the man didn't answer.

Mark kept Kelli to his chest and ran into the hallway. The state of the rest of the cabin confirmed his earlier fear. Someone had not only blown up the side of the house but also set the area around the entire structure on fire. Reason told him that the kitchen and its back door would be their best bet. The figure in the dark wouldn't have had time to get the fire going too strongly there.

Kelli stirred in his arms, coughing violently. He held her tighter and almost yelled in relief when he saw the back door wasn't crawling in flames. He threw it open and ran straight into the water a few yards away. The lake was low for the season, and the dock was high off the water. He splashed under the wood, giving them the only cover available in the backyard.

No shots had rung through the air and no attack had been initiated as they left the house.

But that didn't mean the perpetrator wouldn't still try.

"What the—" Kelli started to catch her breath, eyes open and looking wildly at him.

"Are you okay to stand?" he asked quickly, already tilting her feet into the water. Confused, she nodded. "I need you to stay right here, hidden, okay?"

Again she nodded, but Mark knew it was only a matter of time before she realized her husband wasn't with them. She seemed to still be processing being conscious at the moment. Kelli caught her balance as Mark released her. He pulled his pocketknife from his pants and handed it to her, turning as soon as she grabbed it.

An awful sound filled the air, another in a long line of things that would haunt him about that night.

A fireball erupted from the kitchen and engulfed the rest of the cabin. Glass exploded and the ground shook. The house gave one final wheeze and, together, Mark and Kelli watched as it burned to the ground.

Chapter Two

Kelli slipped off her heels and padded quietly across the floor. Footsteps echoed in the hallway behind her, but she didn't stop. Side-stepping a few boxes left scattered around the room, she hurried into the open closet.

It wasn't deep, but it stretched wide. Empty save a few coat hangers, it didn't allow her much cover. On the other hand she could try to hide behind a stack of boxes in the corner. Though she'd have to really bend to remain hidden. The footsteps came closer, and she had to choose.

The closet would have to do.

Kelli pushed herself to the corner and slid down the wall until she was sitting with her knees pressed up to her chest. The light from the opened bedroom window lit even the mostly dark corner. She would be seen easily by anyone who looked inside the doors.

Silence filled the room.

For a second, Kelli worried. Had she been seen coming into the room? The shuffle of two feet let her know she had. The footsteps came closer, and Kelli held her breath. Her hunter was quick to search around the boxes and move on to the closet. The shuffling stopped a step from the opening. There was a moment of silence that felt almost tangible.

Then a tiny face peeked inside, and Kelli couldn't help but laugh.

"Boo," the little girl yelled. Smiling ear to ear, she squealed in delight as Kelli jumped out of her hiding spot.

"You found me!"

Grace Victoria Crane let out another round of giggles before running off. Kelli laughed as she followed the toddler through the house, knowing the little girl's destination.

Like mother, like daughter, Grace loved the library.

It was her fair-haired beauty's turn to hide.

Behind the wall-length curtains—one of the few things that hadn't yet been packed in the room—stood a pair of little blue shoes. They were covered in sequins, and Kelli knew for a fact that finding them in stock had been a miracle in itself.

"Hmm…" Kelli put her finger to her chin and tapped it. Moving slowly around the boxes and plastic tubs pushed to the side of the room, she made a big show of being confused. "I could have sworn I saw a little girl with chocolate on her mouth run in here!" Grace started to giggle. The sound made Kelli's heart swell. "I wonder who that could be!" She went to the curtains, ready to tickle the culprit, when the little girl jumped out on her own.

"Got you," she yelled. When Grace was excited like this, Kelli couldn't deny the resemblance between them. Although Grace's hair was a shade or two darker, their ever-changing green eyes were almost identical. Her facial features, however, all belonged to her father.

"You're the best hide-and-seeker I think I've ever played with," Kelli said, scooping up the toddler. She was about to unleash another round of tickles when the doorbell chimed. It echoed through the mostly packed up house.

"Me, me," Grace yelled, already trying to wiggle out of her arms and race to answer the door.

"Not without me," Kelli answered. She moved Grace to her hip and took a moment to marvel at how big she was getting. A year and seven months, almost to the day.

The past two years had flown by and yet,

in some ways, Kelli seemed painfully stuck. As she moved down the hallway to the front of the house, she tried to commit to memory how the wood floor felt beneath her bare feet. She wondered what the next year would bring after all of the changes Grace and she were about to make.

A familiar face was bobbing in front of the windows in the front door, inciting a new excitement in Grace. Kelli put her down with a laugh and opened the door for the godmother of her child.

"You're late," Kelli teased Lynn Bradley. The short woman with black hair wore a pair of worn overalls with a long-sleeved yellow flannel shirt that contrasted with her dark skin. Kelli raised her eyebrow at the choice of wardrobe but didn't say anything. Lynn had been a bit eclectic ever since they were children.

"Listen, it's not my fault that you already packed up your TV, forcing me to choose between the end of *You've Got Mail* and the care of your child." The twenty-nine-year-old gave her best friend a smirk before bending down and enveloping Grace in a hug. "My, how you've grown! Look at you! Gosh, how old are you now? Three? Five?"

Grace put her hands on her hips and gave Lynn a critical eye. She held up one finger. "One!"

"That's my girl," Lynn approved. She mussed Grace's hair, and the three of them went inside.

"You were here yesterday, you know," Kelli said as they went into the living room. Lynn laughed.

"That doesn't discount the fact that that kid of yours is growing like crazy! She's going to be taller than me before you know it! She's not two yet and look at her!"

Grace, suddenly uninterested in their conversation, went to her makeshift play area in the corner. It looked like a graveyard for plastic dinosaurs, stuffed animals and Legos.

"I know," Kelli agreed with a smile. It didn't last long. Lynn had come over to help pack up the one room Kelli couldn't get through on her own.

Attached to the living room by a set of French double doors was Victor's home office. It was a small room but had managed to collect a lot of things in the six years he had lived in the house. Just looking into the room had sent Kelli into tears for the first six months after the fire. Then, slowly, she had been able to bear the sight of the room Victor had spent the most time in. Kelli supposed Grace had helped her with that. She had to stay strong for their child, who would never know her father.

Lynn's expression softened, but she didn't comment. Aside from Grace, Lynn had been the most constant part of her world during the past two years.

"Okay, well, let's get started." Kelli motioned to the bookcase. "You empty that and I'll start with the desk."

"Got yah, Boss." Lynn pulled the plastic tub over to the small bookshelf. Although there was a library in the house, the office shelves were filled with research materials collected over Victor's nine-year career as a journalist. Her husband had covered an array of subjects, freelancing from home, and working for newspapers and magazines around the nation. His next goal had been to work internationally, but then they had found out about the pregnancy. Victor had decided his family was more important than work.

Kelli sat down in the office chair, sadness in her heart.

Her thoughts slid back to the night at the cabin.

Sometimes she could still feel the heat of the fire. Smell the smoke in the air. Feel the cold of the water as they waited for help to arrive. The boy behind the fire had been caught, sure, but that didn't make the memories of what had happened any more bearable.

She took a breath. She didn't need to remember that night now.

Ten minutes into packing away the office's contents, Kelli found something she hadn't known existed.

"Hey, look at this."

The middle side drawer of the desk had stuck when she tried to open it. She pulled too hard, and the entire drawer slid out. Along with it came a small notebook that had been taped to the bottom of the drawer above it.

"What is it?" Lynn asked, walking over.

"I don't know. It was hidden."

The notebook wasn't labeled, but it was filled with Victor's pristine handwriting.

"It looks like work notes," Kelli observed. She flipped through it, scanning as she went. "I recognize some of these names…but I thought all of his notes were—" She cut herself off and rephrased. "He took them to the cabin with us. I didn't know he had kept notes here."

Lynn gave her privacy as she thumbed to the last few pages. Possibly the last notes Victor had ever taken. Kelli shook her head. She didn't need to travel down that road today.

"Wait." Her eyes stopped on a passage in neat, tiny writing. "This doesn't make sense."

Or maybe it did.

"WE NEED TO TALK."

Kelli's back was ramrod straight against the office chair. It wasn't made to be comfortable—those who sat across from Dennis Crawford, retired editor of the national online publication known as the *Scale*, didn't usually intend to keep his company long. Especially during house calls like this. She suspected that he had let her in only because of Victor. Dennis and he hadn't been friends, but they'd worked to-gether on more than one occasion.

Including the last story of Victor's life.

"I suspected, considering I haven't seen you since—" He cleared his throat, trying to avoid the fact that their last meeting had been when her husband had been lowered into the ground. Kelli shifted in her seat. "How have you been?" he asked instead.

"Good. Grace is keeping me busy, but I'm sure that won't change for another seventeen years or so."

Dennis, an unmarried man with no children of his own, smiled politely. Victor hadn't told her the man's age, but she placed him in his early forties. Kelli couldn't tell if he was gen-uinely kind, but she could see he carried a lot of self-pride. Although gray was peppered into his black hair, his goatee was meticulous, along with the collared shirt and slacks he wore. Journalism award plaques, athletic trophies, and pictures of Dennis and other men dressed in suits decorated almost every available inch of the home office.

"So, what can I do for you?" His eyes slid down to the folder in her lap. There wasn't any use tiptoeing around what she had come to say.

"I was packing up Victor's office last night when I found some of his old notes." She slid the folder across the desk. "Including these."

Dennis raised an eyebrow—also meticulously kept—but didn't immediately pick up the folder. In that moment she was thankful she'd never had to work under the man. He fixed her with a gaze that clearly said, "So what?"

"They're his notes on the Bowman Foundation story—the last story he covered." That at least made Dennis open the folder, though his eyes stayed on her.

"Okay?" Dennis said.

Kelli shifted in her seat again. "I guess I'm

wondering why the story you printed doesn't match up?"

His eyebrow didn't waver, but his gaze finally dropped to the photocopies she'd made of Victor's notes. The actual notebook was tucked safely into her purse. She didn't want to part with it, not even for a moment. Finding it after the past two years was like finding a small piece of Victor.

"What do you mean, 'doesn't match up?'" Dennis asked, voice defensive. "I used the notes he sent me."

"Not according to *those* notes, which are undoubtedly his." She leaned forward and pointed to the first section she had highlighted. "The names are different. I've already looked them up but can't find anything." Dennis pulled out a drawer and grabbed a pair of glasses from it without saying a word. He slipped them on and leaned his head closer to the paper. From where Kelli sat, she could see his concentration deepen.

But she could also see something else.

Dennis's eyes registered no surprise at what he was seeing.

"Normally I wouldn't second-guess this, but…well, it was his last story," she added.

"The names we published were pulled straight from the email I got from Victor," he said after a minute more of going through the pages. He set his glasses down and threaded his fingers together over the papers. The gesture also looked oddly defensive. "These were probably notes he wrote quickly, then later changed to be accurate. Perhaps it was even his way of brainstorming how he wanted the story to go with placeholder names."

Kelli didn't need to think about that possibility long. She shook her head.

"I think these were his backup notes. He always said he didn't like keeping everything electronically. I just thought his written notes were also with us at the cabin."

Dennis seemed to consider what she said but, by the same token, it felt as though he was putting on a show. What had been an off-balanced feeling of doubt started to turn dark in the pit of her stomach.

"I don't know what to tell you. I personally verified the information—just to be safe—before the piece was published." He shut the folder but didn't slide it back. "The Bowman Foundation publically thanked the *Scale*—and Victor—for the story. Because of the spotlight, they've received a substantial amount of funding since the article debuted. If any of the facts were incorrect, I would have been made aware of it—retired or not."

Kelli considered his words. Was she just overreacting? Was she looking for a reason to revisit the memory of Victor? Had finding his handwritten journal been too much of a shock to her system?

"Listen, Kelli." Dennis's expression softened. He took off his glasses and fixed her with a small smile. "I'm due to meet an old friend for lunch, but how about after that, I'll recheck these." He put his finger on the folder. "I'll call if anything weird pops up."

Despite herself, she smiled, too.

"Thanks. I'd really appreciate it."

Dennis stood, ending the conversation. He moved around the desk and saw her to the front door.

As she turned to thank him again, he said, "I'm sorry about Victor. But, word of advice? Maybe you should start looking to the future and not the past."

Kelli didn't have a lot of memories of her mother, but she knew being polite had been high on her priority list. That thought alone pushed a smile to her lips, while the knot in her stomach tightened. Dennis shut the door, leaving her standing on his porch with a great sense of unease.

You're reading way too into this, Kel, she thought as she turned on her heel. *Calm down and just forget about it all.*

"Hey, Kelli?" Dennis called when she was halfway down his sidewalk. She hadn't heard him open the door. "Do you have the journal those copies were from?"

Her purse suddenly felt heavier at her side. Before she could think about it, she was shaking her head.

"No, I just found the copies."

"Oh, okay, thanks."

She waved bye and continued on her way.

"Because if you did have it, I'd really like to see it," he called after her.

The feeling of unease expanded within her. Once again she turned to face him.

"Sorry. The copies I gave you were all I had."

Dennis shrugged and retreated behind the door. It wasn't until she was safely inside her car that she chanced another look at the house.

It might have been her imagination, but she could almost have sworn the blinds over the living room windows moved.

Chapter Three

Mark cracked his knuckles and swigged a gulp of his beer. Sitting behind the bar of a local dive, he kept his eyes glued to the television screen above him. An old football game was running, but he wasn't paying much attention.

He'd had one heck of a day, if he said so himself.

The construction manager had come in early with a mood that matched the unexpected storm that would mean no work for the next two days to a week. Then the concrete pourer—who had never driven in rain, it seemed—had backed up into Mark's Jeep, breaking a taillight and denting his bumper. The cherry on top was that when he decided to de-stress from an unproductive, unprofitable workday with a drink or two, he'd picked the bar from his past.

"Sorry, I had to take that call." Nikki Waters, founder of the Orion Security Group and his former boss, sat back on her bar stool and reclaimed her drink.

Mark smiled but felt no mirth. He didn't dislike Nikki. In fact, he had once considered her a great friend. However, the past two years had put a weight on the friendship. One that hadn't affected just their relationship but his entire life.

"It's fine," he said, trying to keep his tone light. He remembered meeting Nikki for the first time when she'd been a secretary at Redstone Solutions and he'd been a low-ranking security agent. She'd been quiet, unobtrusive, yet clever and kind. The latter two traits she had held on to, but the first two? Well, he knew from experience that if she was quiet, it was only because she was finding the right words to tell you exactly what was on her mind. And unobtrusive? If she thought people she cared about were making a mistake, she'd tell them.

She'd had *that* talk with Mark several times already in the past year.

"So, how are you, Nik? It's been a while."

The 33-year-old looked surprised he'd made the first conversational move, but she recovered quickly. She straightened her short, dark red ponytail before answering.

"Good. Busy, but good." She motioned to the bar around them. "I would actually still be at the office, but the storm knocked out our power. Jonathan told me it was a sign we needed to 'capitalize on Friday night.'" Mark mentally winced at the mention of Jonathan. Along with Nikki and Oliver Quinn, Jonathan Carmichael rounded out friends with whom he had all but severed ties since he left Orion. "I'd heard him talk about this place on more than one occasion, so I thought I'd give it a try."

"The service isn't great, but I can't complain about the price."

Nikki laughed. "I'll drink to that." And she did.

"What about you? How've you been?"

"Good," he lied. "Not as busy, but okay. Working with a decent construction crew on a neighborhood south of the hospital. Keeps my muscles working," he joked. Nikki laughed again, but it was laced with concern.

"Listen, Mark," she started, but he cut her off.

"I don't want to come back, Nikki. I told you then that I was done with being a bodyguard, and I still mean it now."

"But, Mark, you have also told me before how much you love it," she pointed out. "You can't let one incident deter you."

"Incident?" he repeated. "A man died, Nik."

"It wasn't your fault. I don't know how many times everyone has to tell you that."

"My one job was to keep him safe, and instead I let some punk kid burn him alive." His voice rose as he said it, and the bartender shot him a look that clearly asked him to settle down. Nikki didn't flinch. This fight was an old one by now. He couldn't help it, though. Every time he thought about Darwin McGregor—the firebug—and his floundering admission to the cops that he had set fire to the cabin for fun, Mark's mood instantly turned heated. The nineteen-year-old had said that blowing up the large propane tank had been nothing more than an accident. He'd thought the tank was empty. He'd thought no one would be hurt, just scared. It didn't change the fact that Victor had died.

Or that Mark didn't believe him.

Images of the dark figure running away from the house flashed through his mind. He had been too tall and too wide to be Darwin. Though the cops, Nikki and everyone else had blamed this accusation on Mark's overwhelming guilt.

It was another reason he had quit Orion six months later.

"Yes, it's our job to protect people," she said, lowering her voice in an attempt to get him to do the same. "But that doesn't mean we can be everywhere at once." She stretched her hand out as if to touch his but stopped. "It was a horrible accident, yet even Mrs. Crane agreed that her husband's death wasn't your fault. You saved a woman and her unborn child. That has to count for something."

Mark took another swig of his beer.

"Don't you think we've talked about this enough already, Nik?" he asked, adjusting his voice back to a tone he thought was pleasant.

Again she started to say something but caught herself before nodding. She reached into her pocket and pulled out an Orion business card. There was a number already written across its back in pen. She slid it over to him.

"You're right. I'm sorry. This will be the last time I bring any of this up," she promised.

"What's this?" He nodded to the card. He didn't recognize the number.

"Let me preface this. I didn't want to tell you, considering everything you've been through, but she insisted she needed to talk to you."

Mark was perplexed. "Who needs to talk to me?"

"Kelli Crane."

Mark's mouth dropped open slightly. "Why?" he asked. "And when did she call?"

"I'm not sure why—I didn't ask and she didn't offer the information up—but she called a few hours ago." Nikki waved the bartender over. "All she said was that she found something you might be able to help her with."

"I—I have no idea what she's talking about," Mark said more to himself than his former boss.

"Then you might want to call her back." She

smiled and handed her credit card over to clear out her tab. It sobered Mark.

"I find it hard to believe that you happened to take a message for me on the same day you just happened to run into me at a bar. Did you come here to give this to me?"

Her smile grew wide. "Let's just say, I'm hitting two birds with one stone." She gave the man a pat on the shoulder. "It was good to see you, Mark. I hope everything works out."

"Thanks, Nik. You, too."

Mark stared down at the number after she'd gone. It was amazing how ten digits could affect him so profoundly. He quickly looked around the bar, as if the patrons could hear his internal struggle. No one paid him any mind. He slipped the card into his jacket.

Less than an hour later, Mark was sitting in his apartment, staring at his phone. There was nothing to be afraid of about calling Kelli. She had, after all, wanted to talk to him. But Mark couldn't get past the why of it all. Why call? Why now?

"Only one way to find out," he announced to the empty room.

Mark dialed the number before realizing how late it was. He didn't know her child's name but knew she lived with Kelli. The last thing he needed was another reason for Kelli to be upset with him. Waking up her toddler was something he wanted to avoid if possible. He hung up on the third ring, deciding to call her the next day.

Again, he wondered why she wanted to talk to him.

Mark waited around for a few more minutes before deciding to take a shower. It was quick and refreshing, a great contrast to a not-so-great day. His new mood stuck as he got to his phone and saw he had a voice mail.

The number matched the one Nikki had given

him. He put the message on speaker and listened as Kelli Crane's voice echoed off the walls.

"Mark Tranton? Hi, this is Kelli Crane. There's something I really need to talk to you about. Can we meet? Let me know." She paused. Mark almost ended the recording before she said one last thing.

"I don't think Victor's death was an accident."

THE NEXT WORKDAY was a washout, just as Mark had thought it would be. Thanks to a heavy rain in the middle of the night before, his construction site and crew were put on hold. That could have been a time to relax for Mark—they'd been working long hours before the storm came in—but he still wouldn't entertain the idea of a vacation. He was the kind of man who not only appreciated hard work but also craved it. When that work stopped, for whatever reason, he was left with a world of thought he'd rather not visit. So instead of lounging around—or, heaven forbid, sleeping in—Mark changed into his sweats and hit the gym.

The workout room was sectioned off in the corner of the bottom floor of his apartment complex, which gave the place a solitude that Mark liked. Or maybe it was the feeling of improvement that working out brought him. Either way, it was a ritual he could do anywhere, whenever he wanted. He didn't need permission. He didn't need advice.

Whether or not he was a bodyguard didn't matter.

"I don't think Victor's death was an accident."

Mark brought his fist back from the speed bag. Kelli Crane's admission had all but stopped him from breathing. Not because it was out of left field. No, because it was strange to hear his theory come out of the widow's mouth.

A theory that had been thrown aside by everyone he'd cared about and thought cared about him. Even Nikki had tried to talk him out of it until she'd been blue in the face. She was trying to protect him from himself, she'd said. But all she'd done was shown him that at the end of the day maybe she didn't believe in him as much as he'd once thought.

His fist connected with the bag again. He could feel the teeth of the past sinking back into him, and he had two options. Try to pry them off or ignore them until he couldn't feel their sting.

The second option had treated him well the past year. He snorted, knowing that was a lie.

Mark went through his boxing routine, trying to drown out his thoughts, but each time his skin connected with the bag, he seemed to fall deeper down the hole. The image of the mystery culprit—not the nineteen-year-old firebug—flashed across his mind.

"Whoa, what did the bag ever do to you?" Mark spun around to find his neighbor Craig go for the weights. He was grinning, but his smile fell when he saw Mark's face. "Everything okay?"

Mark realized his breathing had become rapid, his heart beating fast. His shirt clung to his chest, sweat keeping it flat against his torso. A dull ache in his hands began to register.

"Just blowing off some steam," he said, changing his harsh tone to one that could pass as conversational. It worked well enough.

"You already have steam? The sun just came up!" Craig laughed. "Must be about a woman."

Mark shrugged. "You could say that."

They talked about the weather and their jobs for a while before doing their own things. Mark's hands finally begged him to give it a rest, so he said bye to Craig and huffed back to his third-floor apartment.

It wasn't a big space—a studio with a box of

a balcony—but Mark didn't need much. The only mementos he truly treasured were the pictures that hung on the walls. His parents and younger sister, Beth; friends from his hometown in Florida; and even one that had been taken the day Orion had officially opened. That one, though, he didn't really look at anymore. The rest of his valuables consisted of his home media center and laptop—both of which he had seldom used since starting his construction job. A homey place it was not, but it sufficed.

Mark walked to the glass door that led to the balcony and looked out. It was a cloudy seventy degrees and was expected to get chilly. A cold front was supposedly blowing in that night, but he wasn't about to put stock in anything the forecast projected. In his ten years of Dallas living, he had learned that if you didn't like the weather in Texas, you should just wait an hour. It often changed.

The quiet of his apartment crept around him

the longer he stood there. He hadn't called Kelli back, and he didn't know if he would. After Victor had died—and in the year that followed—he had almost gone crazy following his gut, trying to find the figure in the dark who had started the fire. Even after Darwin McGregor admitted that it had been him.

Determination had turned into obsession. Walls went up around him as each of his friends tried to tell him it was his guilt that fueled the pursuit. Nothing more and nothing less. Then, on the one-year anniversary of the fire, he had decided it was time to let it go.

This was the first time, however, that Kelli had ever mentioned it.

He eyed his phone on the coffee table. Didn't he owe it to her to at least hear her out?

Chapter Four

The weatherman might not have been completely wrong. As Mark stepped out of his taxi, he wondered if he should have brought his jacket. His long sleeves might not cut it if the temperature dropped even further.

It was just after dinner, and he was back at the bar he'd been at the night before. He had a feeling the place would be seeing a lot of him in the next few weeks, especially if this meeting went south. He'd finally called Kelli back and was surprised when she'd asked to meet him somewhere later that night. Nothing more was said beyond that, and now here he was,

showing up a half hour early. Nerves or anticipation? He couldn't tell which, but he made his
way to one of the booths tucked into the corner.
It gave him a clear sightline to the front doors.

From habit, he took in his surroundings. Men
and women of varying careers were all dressed
down to some degree—one of the women at
the table next to him had on flats, though a
pair of heels could be seen sticking out of the
bag at her feet, while the other had let her hair
loose across her shoulders; an older man at the
bar had his tie undone around his neck, beer
in hand and eyes on the TV; a group of yup-
pies had their blazers draped over chair backs
while they threw darts next to the front door;
a man walked in and immediately went to the
bar, hand up, ordering a beer.

A few more patrons came in and before he
knew it, the half hour had passed. Mark hadn't
spent enough time with Kelli Crane to know if
she was punctual or not.

No, he didn't really know her at all.

The Orion Security Group had done its homework on the now twenty-nine-year-old woman before the contract had started. It was imperative to do the research to make the protection side of the job most effective. He'd learned that Kelli Crane—formally McKinnely—had a degree in art therapy and worked with the elderly at the community center. She came from a small family that all but disappeared after a car crash killed her parents when she was young. Socially she had kept out of the spotlight, staying close with a childhood friend named Lynn.

In that regard, she was quite the opposite of her late husband. Victor Crane had been a networker, thanks to his job. He had more connections than even Orion's analyst had been able to uncover. Mark had tracked down as many as he could, trying to find a tie between the man's death and the fire, but it was hard to find a link when you didn't know what you were looking for in the first place.

Mark couldn't help but focus on the blonde as she paused to survey the room before meeting his gaze. There was no hesitation in her bright eyes. She made a beeline for him.

Although he'd recognized her easily, he had to admit she looked different from the woman he'd known through the contract. Kelli walked with unmistakable purpose. Her once-long hair was shortened to her chin with bangs that cut straight over her eyebrows. The dirty blond had lightened as her skin had darkened—she'd been getting sun. He'd bet her kid had something to do with that. Instead of the almost prim outfits she had worn at the cabin, she was dressed more casually—a blue button-up with jeans and black flats. There was no flashy jewelry—he noticed no wedding ring, either—and even her purse seemed more practical than pretty.

Seeing her made him wonder what he looked like in turn. Had he changed in the past two years?

"Hi," Kelli greeted him, sliding into the seat across from him without pause. Whatever was on her mind, it had her determined.

"Hi," he responded. Mark didn't know what to feel, seeing her so informally, as if they were old friends reconnecting. The only thing they shared was a tragedy. Did she feel the same self-loathing he did?

"Thanks for meeting me, by the way. I know it must be strange."

"It's the least I can do." He cleared his throat. "So, how have you been?"

"Good. Busy, but good."

Mark smiled. It was the same thing he'd said to Nikki the day before. He wondered if Kelli actually meant it.

In record time, the waitress popped over and took her drink order before they could dive in to their conversation. Kelli asked for beer and cracked a big smile. Mark couldn't help but raise his eyebrow at her expression.

"Sorry. I haven't gotten out much since Grace." She tamped her grin down a fraction. "And I certainly haven't been to a bar and ordered beer. I almost feel like this is a mini-vacation." Her smile instantly vanished, like a candle blown out. Silence followed as she dropped her gaze.

"Kelli, why did you want to meet?"

The blonde quirked her lips to one side as she concentrated. She was choosing her words carefully. Finally she found them.

"After the fire, the cops came. You told them you'd seen a man running from the house," she started. This time she didn't shy away from his gaze. "When they picked up Darwin McGregor—" she paused, eyes momentarily glazing over with emotion "—you said it wasn't the same person. At the time I didn't even think to question it—he admitted to setting the fire—but now..."

"But now?" he pressed.

"Well, I think I should have listened to you."

Mark was an impassive man. He didn't know if that was what had made him such a good bodyguard—before the fire—or if it had been the other way around. Sure, like anyone, he had emotions. He felt things like the next man. It was his ability to mask those feelings, those shifts in conversation that surprised him, that he had mastered through the years. However, as the words left Kelli Crane's mouth, once again he had to struggle to keep from gaping.

Not so much at their meaning. It was the implication behind them.

"I don't understand," he said honestly.

Kelli's drink arrived, but she didn't touch it. Her minivacation was apparently over.

"The story Victor was working on at the cabin—did you ever read it?"

"No." Mark didn't want to lie, but he also didn't want to admit why he hadn't. He'd tried before but even the headline had made his guilt expand. Reading the article was salt on the wound of not being able to save the man. If Kelli was offended, she didn't show it.

"The Bowman Foundation, a charity, had been operating anonymously in Texas for a few years but decided to go public. Victor did an in-depth spotlight on them—what they had already accomplished, what they hoped to accomplish, that sort of thing." She moved her hand to hover over her purse but paused before placing it back on the tabletop. "It was published a week after the funeral." Her smile was weak at the word. "While I was packing— we're moving to a new house— I found Victor's journal with a copy of his notes about the story. Now I've read the published article over and over again. I've memorized every detail."

"Okay…I'm not following."

"The two don't match up." He could tell she was getting frustrated, but at what or whom, he wasn't sure.

"The published story and the notes?" he asked.

Kelli nodded. "Names, not important in the grand scheme of the foundation."

Mark took a drink of his beer. "So they got the facts wrong. What does this have to do with anything?"

Kelli's fists balled slightly, a move that someone else might have missed entirely. Mark was suddenly aware of *how* aware he was of Kelli's movements.

"I talked to the editor of the *Scale*. He says it was Victor who was wrong, but I don't believe that. Victor was using that spotlight to show he was capable of writing more feature articles. He figured it would help him get local work so he wouldn't have to travel as much when Grace came. He wouldn't have made *that* many errors."

"I'm sorry, but I'm still not following."

When she continued, her voice was noticeably lower.

"I think Victor might have stumbled across something that he shouldn't have…and was killed for it."

MARK'S EYEBROWS STAYED STILL, and his lips remained in their detached frown, but Kelli saw a twinge of movement in his jaw. He was trying to pretend he didn't have a reaction to her accusation, but she'd seen it clear as day. She thanked two years of people trying to hide their pity for the widowed mother. She'd seen *that* look so many times that she had learned to read when most people were trying to hide what they really felt.

Mark had a reaction, but she didn't know what emotion was behind it.

"Do you have any evidence to back that up?" he asked, voice even. "Aside from the difference between notes."

Kelli remembered Dennis Crawford's sharp stare as his hand stayed firmly on the photocopies she'd brought to him.

"Have you ever had a gut feeling, Mark? One that starts out as a tiny doubt and then grows and grows until you can't ignore it anymore?"

"Yes," he admitted. "But having a gut feeling can only take you so far. What you're trying to say is someone targeted and killed Victor. You need more than a gut feeling to back that up."

"But aren't you convinced that Darwin didn't start that fire? What about the man you saw running from the cabin that night?"

Mark took a long second before he said, "Darwin admitted to it. Why would he do that if he didn't actually start it?"

"Maybe he was put up to it. Maybe he was threatened. Maybe—"

"Kelli." Mark's jaw definitely hardened, along with his tone. She must have reacted, because just as quickly he softened. "It was an accident."

"But you—"

Mark's set his beer down hard. "I was wrong, Kelli." The women next to them glanced over. He cleared his throat. "I'm sorry, but I can't help you with this."

It was an unmistakable end to the conversation.

Just as the pity of strangers had taught Kelli to read subtle reactions, her daughter had taught her the face of stubborn resolve.

"Then I'm sorry to have wasted your time." She pulled out some cash to cover her untouched beer. "Thanks again for meeting me. Good night."

Mark looked like he wanted to say something, but he didn't. Kelli left the table without a look back, not even pausing as she brushed shoulders with a man leaving the bar.

Her face was hot and the outside air did little to cool it down. The heat came from either embarrassment at not being believed, or anger for the same reason. Maybe a mixture of both. Or, maybe her emotion wasn't even meant for the ex-bodyguard.

Kelli took a deep breath.

Seeking out the only person who ever suspected foul play, and to have even him turn you down...

She let the breath out.

You really are overreacting.

Kelli followed the sidewalk, passing back by one of the bar's open windows. The farther away she walked, the more convinced she became that the whole conspiracy was in her head. Moving out of the only home she'd ever had with Victor while juggling work and Grace was a lot of stress to carry. She thought she'd been handling it well enough, especially with Lynn's help, but maybe she hadn't.

Time to put it behind you, Kel.

"Don't make a noise." The harsh command came beside her ear just as a sharp point dug into her shirt. A large hand grabbed her upper arm. Kelli's stomach dropped as her heart began to gallop. Before she had time to decide if she was or wasn't going to comply, the man yanked her into a nearby alley. It was empty. No one yelled after them. "Turn around and I cut you," the voice growled. "Make one move or sound and I cut you. Got it?"

Kelli felt her head bob up and down. She was facing the brick wall of a business she couldn't remember at the moment. Her mind filled with images of Grace. The thought of her child put a bit of spirit back into her, but not enough for her to be careless.

"Drop your purse," the low voice ground out.

Kelli slowly raised the arm that he wasn't

holding and maneuvered the strap off her chest and shoulder. She tried to gauge the size of the knife, but her nerves were too frazzled. The purse was on the ground for less than a second before the man snatched it back up. She saw his black-gloved hand. It made the terror in her rise even more.

Instead of leaving, he applied more pressure with the knife. She winced but didn't make a noise.

"There. That wasn't so hard, was it?" His breath brushed against her ear. It sent a chill up her spine.

"You have what you wanted," she said, voice shaking.

The knife bit deeper. This time she let out a small yelp.

"Didn't I say *no talki*—"

"I have a gun," interrupted a cool voice from even farther behind her, definitely not her original attacker. "Hurt her and I'll—"

Kelli was pushed into the wall as the man let go of her arm and struggled with the newcomer. Pain burst in her cheek as it scraped the brick. She didn't pause to check it. She braced herself against the wall as she turned around.

Her attacker was a white man—she couldn't guess an age well enough—dressed in all denim and black with a red baseball cap. He wasn't tall but he was wide. In one hand he held her purse. The other was busy trying to fend off her savior.

Who just happened to be Mark Tranton.

"Give me the purse," Mark commanded. His arm was cut, but he was holding a knife. Apparently having a gun had been a bluff.

The mugger eyed what used to be his weapon before darting to the left and out of the alley, taking the purse with him. For a large man, he was lithe.

"Are you okay?" Mark asked, eyes roaming her over.

"Yeah," she breathed.

And then he was running.

Chapter Five

The man was fast. Like a jackrabbit, he cut across the road and disappeared into an alley opposite them with impressive speed. Mark was more of a hand-to-hand combat guy, but he held his own, only slowing down when a Mazda didn't brake, apparently not worried about hitting pedestrians.

He chased the mugger through the network of alleys that connected two blocks. Dumpsters lined the sides and debris littered the ground, but the man used neither to try to block or slow Mark down. Instead, he ran full tilt. Which meant Mark wasn't going to catch him unless he got creative.

His memory began to pull an aerial layout of the alleyways. The one they were running down had three turnoffs before forking into two paths. One went left into another busy downtown block, next to a chic restaurant that stayed open until midnight. The other torqued right between a Chinese take-out joint and a boutique. The way the man was running, he seemed set on a destination. He hadn't hesitated when passing the first two turnoffs.

Mark didn't, either.

He didn't break speed as he skidded around into the first turnoff and ran the length of the short alley. It deposited him back onto a less busy sidewalk where businesses were darkened for the night. A few bystanders too drunk to drive and too broke to call a taxi dotted the sidewalks. Mark spun around a couple that stood and gawked at him. His breathing hitched at the extra movement, but he knew his body could handle the chase. He might not have been a bodyguard anymore, but he'd never stopped training.

The stretch of block ended, and he cut left around a closed café on the corner. Pumping his legs harder, he made it to the mouth of the alley.

It was empty.

"Dammit!"

Mark spun around, his eyes darting to all escape routes. There was no hurried motion on the sidewalks. None of the people milling around seemed alarmed. The mugger hadn't come out of the alley. Mark had misjudged.

Or had he?

With the knife heavy in his hand, Mark reentered the alley. He kept his body loose, ready to move if the other man jumped out. But no one did. He paused, listening for another set of footsteps, before bending to pick up what had caught his eye.

It was Kelli's purse.

BACKTRACKING THROUGH THE alley to the bar, Mark kept an eye out for security cameras or any obvious eyewitnesses who might have caught the face of the mugger. There were neither. He put the knife in his pocket as he neared the street; the bag was secured underneath his arm.

"Mark!" Kelli was standing outside the bar again with a manager he knew. The older man had a phone to his ear and nodded to Mark before retreating back into the business. Kelli waved him over. The obvious relief that painted her face at the sight of him made him uneasy.

"I think this belongs to you," he said by way of greeting. Kelli took her purse, but her eyes stayed on his.

"Thank you." The expression of relief turned

to gratitude. Again, it made him uneasy. He nodded.

"Are you okay?" he motioned to her cheek. It was red, scraped, with a few spots of blood.

"Yeah. I'd rather have this than a cut from the knife." She quieted.

"Did the manager call the cops?"

"Yes. When you took off, I ran back to call. I would have used my cell phone, but it's in my purse." That's when she noticed the cut on his arm. He could feel its sting but knew it was harmless. "You're hurt!"

"Don't worry. It looks worse than it feels."

"Hey, you get a good look at the guy?" The manager had come back out without the phone. Mark didn't miss the bulge of a gun beneath his shirt.

"Not his face," he admitted. "But I do know he was sitting at your bar."

"He was in the bar?" Kelli asked, voice pitching high. The manager didn't seem too thrilled, either. Even in the dim light from the street lamp, Mark could see his face redden in anger.

"He was sitting at the end closest to the corner. I remember seeing the back of his jacket. He got up as soon as you passed him, leaving. He seemed a little too interested, so I thought I'd check it out." He looked at the manager. "He had a beer in his hand, so—"

"So we have him on camera. And maybe his card is on file, too," the man finished. "A cop is on the way. He'll want your statement, so you two stick around. A beer on the house for your troubles."

"Thanks," Kelli said, though she didn't follow the man back inside. Her attention was on her purse.

"Hundreds of muggings a year and you have the luck of the draw to get one of them," Mark said.

That pulled a snort from her. "Bad luck seems to follow me."

Whether she meant it to be a pointed comment or an off-the-cuff response, it sobered him. Standing a few inches shorter than him, Kelli looked suddenly fragile. He had to remind himself she was the same woman who'd stood her ground and kept calm when a lowlife punk had a knife pulled on her.

"What did he take?" he asked, not wanting to think about what might have happened had he not followed them.

Her eyebrow arched. "Nothing," she answered.

"What?"

She produced her wallet and phone.

"Okay, now *that's* lucky right there!"

"Is it?" Kelli's expression turned skeptical fast. "Why not take *anything*?" she asked. Opening her wallet, she showed him it was full of cash.

"I must have scared him off."

"Or—"

Her thought was cut off as a police cruiser pulled up behind them. The officer got out, and Mark went to meet him. This definitely wasn't how he'd anticipated the night going.

Twenty minutes later, Kelli was ready to go home. The officer took their statements and then went to look at the security footage with the manager. Mark wanted to go, too, but he couldn't see the reason behind it. Kelli was safe and had her belongings back.

"Are you sure you're okay?" Mark asked as they got to her car. Sudden guilt riddled him. The first time he'd seen her since the fire and she'd been attacked.

"I'm fine," she said with a kind, polite smile. "Thanks for everything, Mark."

They didn't say much more. Just the awkward goodbye two relative strangers exchanged without committing to seeing each other again. Mark watched as she drove away.

He was surprised at how the thought of never seeing her again struck a sour note.

Then, just as the feeling occurred, guilt followed it.

"I'M FINE."

It was the second time Kelli had said it within the space of an hour, but this time it was to a very anxious Lynn. Her best friend was sprawled across the couch with a magazine open on her lap, and her eyes were saucers.

"Oh, my God, I can't believe you got mugged!"

"Hey, quiet. My kid's trying to sleep," Kelli warned with a smile. Seeing Lynn so obviously upset was starting to make her calm crack. She was surprised she had even been able to recount the entire story before Lynn interrupted.

"I know she's asleep," Lynn said, dropping the volume of her voice. "I'm the one who put her there and read that annoying counting-sheep book to her. Can we just get rid of that thing, by the way? Maybe 'misplace' it? Say the Easter Bunny needed it to keep on hopping, or maybe Santa needed it to fight crime or something? I think I've read that to her at least a hundred times already."

Kelli appreciated Lynn's attempt to calm her with a change of subject. The knotted stress within her lessened. She kicked off her shoes and leaned back into the pillows.

"And risk a never-ending tantrum? No way. I'd rather read it every night than endure *one* night without it."

Lynn seemed to reconsider her stance before returning to the topic at hand.

"I still can't believe you got jumped." Her face softened, lips turning down. "He could have really hurt you, Kel."

"I know, but he didn't."

Lynn's eyes slid to the scrape on her cheek. As Kelli had sat in the driveway outside the house, the light from the car mirror had shown her the small wound looked worse than it felt. Which is what Mark had said of his cut. Her thoughts switched to the man.

"I'm just glad Mark saw the guy follow me out," she admitted out loud. "Do you know he didn't even have a gun on him? The only weapon he had, he *took* from the guy."

Lynn whistled. "He's got my praise. So how *was* talking to the bodyguard after all this time? What did he want to talk to you about?" Out of all of the people who had ever stepped into Kelli's life, Lynn was the one person she'd always confided in without hesitation. From the crush she'd had on Billy Ryan in third grade to that one thing Victor had done in bed, there had never been a wall between them.

Until Kelli had found Victor's journal and started to investigate.

The urge to tell Lynn of her suspicions had been great, but something had stopped her. Whether that was fear of judgment or embarrassment at making something out of nothing, Kelli wasn't sure. Regardless, the excuse she'd made to meet Mark had been a lie.

"It was good. Nothing too special, just catching up." Another lie. Another shot of guilt. "But he's no longer a bodyguard," she added, needing a dose of truth to ease her conscience.

"What do you mean?"

"He quit last year." Nikki had told her that when she had called looking for him.

"Why?"

Kelli shrugged, but she could bet why he'd quit security. She couldn't ignore the way Nikki had sounded almost sad as she recounted the information.

Lynn switched subjects again. They talked about the latest episode of *The Bachelor*—which sidetracked them to the topic of Lynn's new neighbor, who had a "smoking body" but "not so much personality." Eventually both women's eyes started to shut, so they said good-night.

"Don't forget to let that kid of yours know who got sent home from my show," Lynn said at the door.

"You let her watch it?" Kelli asked, ready to admonish her. Lynn kept walking away with a wave.

"Just tell her it was the guy with the silly shirt. She'll know what I'm talking about."

Kelli laughed and shut the door after Lynn was safe in her car. She bumped her hip against the door to make sure it was shut all the way, threw the deadbolt and turned off the porch light. The cold of the hardwood floor made her pause. Moving across town to be closer to Lynn—and in a more affordable place—was definitely a move she needed to make, but…

She placed her hand on the door. It was polished and perfect. It reminded her of Victor picking her up and walking her over the threshold when they first got back from their honeymoon. He had insisted, even though they'd been living together for months.

Memories like that made her heart heavy as she walked through the house.

Heavy with love.

Heavy with loss.

She dropped her hand from the door and let out a long breath. Just because she was leaving didn't mean she was leaving the memories, too. With a weird ache tearing through her emotions, Kelli decided to go to the one place that often helped soothe the rising grief.

Since Grace's bedroom was mostly boxed up, the toddler had been sharing the king-size bed with her mom. Though the bed never seemed big enough if Grace got into a good dream. Kelli stood in the doorway and watched as the fair-haired child slept peacefully, unaware of her mother's tumultuous thoughts. The ache within her began to dissipate.

Without undressing, she climbed into bed next to the girl, wrapping her arms around her. Grace—a snuggler—burrowed closer to her.

You're okay, Kel. You've got all you need right here.

But even as she drifted to sleep, letting go of the hectic night's worries, Kelli couldn't help but pinpoint the one fact that felt off about her night's bad luck.

Why hadn't the mugger taken anything?

In the haze between wakefulness and sleep, her thoughts went to Victor's journal, hidden in a box in the kitchen.

Maybe he'd been looking for something more specific.

Chapter Six

Guilt hung heavy within Mark's chest. Lying in bed, he couldn't get the image of Kelli's scraped cheek out of his head. What was it about the Cranes that nulled his ability to keep them safe? It was a question that had pushed itself to the front of his mind during his cab ride home the night before…and it had still been there when he awoke.

"Get it together, Tranton," he scolded himself. "The past is the past." But even as he said it, he knew it wasn't true. The past had called him back to his favorite bar, asking him to avenge a man who died because of him.

The weather forecast was clear for today, but a storm was in the distance. He could smell the rain as he walked to his small balcony. Drought for months and then nothing but rain. Dallas was consistent with its weather inconsistency.

He moved through his apartment, trying to focus on anything other than last night. It wasn't working.

"Have you ever had a gut feeling, Mr. Tranton?"

Yes.

That Darwin McGregor wasn't behind the fire.

But he wasn't in the business of trusting his gut. Not anymore. Not when it hadn't even twinged at the cabin that night.

Mark skipped his morning gym session and went straight for the shower. He managed to wipe his mind of any thoughts of the past. So much so that when he got out and looked at himself in the mirror, he took a moment to shave. Jonathan Carmichael would have been proud. Every time they had worked together during their time at Redstone Solutions or the Orion Security Group, he had always commented on Mark's five-o'clock shadow and lack of neatness. Facial hair hadn't been a point of fixation for the ex-bodyguard, and that had driven Jonathan a little crazy.

"You look like you're the one we're protecting our client from."

The memory made him snort.

And now I don't protect anyone.

His hand paused midmotion.

Once he had shaved, he decided Jonathan would've approved—he did have to admit it made him look better. He was heading to the bedroom when a knock sounded at the apartment door.

Eyeing the buzzer on the kitchen wall, he quickly went through a list of people already in the building who would want to pay him a visit.

He wasn't pals with any of the tenants, but on occasion he would get asked to watch the game or go out drinking with Craig from the gym. As he walked to the door, towel around his waist, chest still bare, he marveled at the fact that he couldn't even recall Craig's last name.

Which was fine, since it was Kelli waiting at the door for him.

"Oh," he said, opening the door wide from its original cracked position.

"Oh," she repeated. Her eyes darted up and down his body. He pictured the pair of shorts and shirt on his bed that he probably should have put on before answering the door. "Sorry. Is this a bad time?" she asked, recovering. A slow pink had risen in her cheeks.

"No. I just got out of the shower." He motioned to the towel that hung low on his hips, just in case the droplets of water across his bare skin and his wet hair weren't enough proof to make his claim believable.

"Right. Um, could I maybe talk to you for a minute? I promise it won't take long."

Mark stepped back and waved her inside, cautious of how loose the towel felt as he moved. After everything they'd been through, he didn't think flashing Kelli Crane was the best way to start a conversation.

"Make yourself comfortable. Let me go get dressed."

Kelli nodded and took a seat on the couch, but only on the edge of it. She was uncomfortable, but why? Mark dressed in record time and sat in a chair across from the intriguing young woman, ready to find out.

"Sorry if coming by was too intrusive," she started. "I may have Googled your number the other night, trying to find your address." The blush from earlier came back, but not as strong. "I was in the neighborhood, meeting my realtor for some papers, when I realized how close your apartment is. So I decided dropping by might be better than leaving another voice mail." She gave a little laugh. "Now I see that maybe it was just creepier."

Mark still wasn't sure he could sum up how he felt at seeing Kelli again—especially in his apartment, wearing a pair of tight jeans and a form-fitting blouse—but he didn't feel creeped out in the least. He hadn't even thought to ask her yet how she'd gotten into the building.

"It's not creepy," he admitted. "But I am curious how you got in without buzzing up."

"A man asked me who I was here to see and waved me in." Her smile was small. "Said he was worried you hadn't shown up for the gym that morning."

He laughed. He really needed to learn Craig's last name.

"So what's up?" Mark asked when it was clear she needed a bit of prodding. "Did they catch the mugger?"

Kelli shook her head. "They told me they'd

call if they did, but so far, no call. That's partly why I wanted to talk." She readjusted in her seat and seemed to take a breath before looking him in the eye. "I wanted to sincerely apologize for everything. I shouldn't have asked you to meet me after all this time just to spin a paranoid theory about a charity, of all places. I just— I guess I thought I'd accepted—to some degree—what happened to Victor. Finding his journal showed me that maybe I haven't fully."

She shrugged, sudden vulnerability showing in each movement. "After I had Grace, I needed to be strong for her—for us—to make it. I suppose I might have buried some feelings rather than faced them. Though creating a conspiracy in my head was probably the wrong route to take."

Her gray-green eyes took on a new shade as the conversation left the past behind. The vulnerable side of Kelli disappeared with it. The corner of her lips pulled up into a smile. "To apologize for trying to rope you into my crazy, I'd like to invite you to dinner tonight at my house. And before you say yes or no, I should warn you—my best friend, Lynn, will be there, and, of course, Grace. Most of the house is boxed up. So if you're expecting fancy, you won't find it there."

Mark tightened his jaw so his mouth didn't fall open in surprise. Once again, he hadn't expected their conversation to go the way it had. Being invited into Kelli's home to eat with her loved ones? No, he hadn't seen that invitation coming.

And he didn't know how to feel about it, either.

"Listen, I appreciate the offer—I really do—but you don't owe me anything, Kelli. You don't have to apologize to me." *Ever*, he wanted to add.

The blonde's smile grew. "Now, you listen to me. You saved me last night, and…well, it wasn't the first time." She pulled a small piece of paper out of her purse and handed it to him before standing. "I'd really appreciate it if you came, Mark. I'd feel a whole lot better knowing that—after I'd gone a bit crazy—you at least got a good meal out of it." She started to walk to the door before pausing. "Unless you already had plans? I—I realize I didn't even ask." Kelli's eyes quickly flicked toward the bedroom.

He smiled. "No plans here," he said.

"Okay, great. Then you really have no excuse not to come." That made him laugh. Kelli Crane was tenacious.

"Fine," he replied, copying her playful tone. "I'll be there with bells and whistles on."

Kelli's expression contorted to disgust. "I know that that's an expression but please, dear goodness, don't bring bells or whistles into my house. I have a toddler. She will want them and use them until we've all gone crazy."

Mark laughed again and followed her to the door. "Deal."

Kelli smiled and was gone, leaving him standing in his doorway with the paper in his hand. On it was an address and the starting time of seven. His eyes went back to the house number, and his memory sparked. Guilt undid the fun humor he'd lapsed into with Kelli when he realized she still lived in the same house she'd shared with Victor.

He was about to go to the house of the man he'd let die, to eat with his widow and daughter.

Mark rubbed the back of his neck.

He'd spent the past year trying to keep away from the past, and here he was, going to dinner with it.

LYNN HAD HER face so close to the window that her breathing was starting to fog up the glass. Grace, who had been copying her godmother's nosiness minutes before, was now sitting next to her feet, playing with Lynn's phone. Kelli rolled her eyes and wiped sauce off her hand onto a dish towel. She was a decent cook but lousy at keeping the ingredients off her. She wouldn't be packing the dish towels until they were out the door and on to the new house.

"You know, typically, when you invite guests to dinner, you're not supposed to watch for them so intensely," Kelli said. "That's what the doorbell is for. It lets you know when your invitee arrives."

Lynn turned her head and rolled her eyes. "First, don't act like you invite people over all of the time," she said, serious. "Second, I'm sorry if I'm insanely curious about the person you *did* finally invite over."

Kelli kept her smile firmly on her lips. They both knew the reason she hadn't been the most entertaining woman in the past year. Being a single working parent had limited her time. As far as her first guest being a man, well, that had surprised her, too.

Inviting Mark over hadn't been an impulsive decision. Instead, it had been one that grew from a thought seeded in her mind during the moments right before sleep. It wasn't until she was driving to meet the Realtor that she'd decided to act on the idea. Despite short notice, Lynn had been more than willing to help keep Grace entertained while they all ate. Even though Kelli had explained she truly needed to apologize and show thanks to Mark for saving her the night before, Lynn liked to tease her. She'd done it when Kelli wouldn't admit she'd liked Martin Ballard their sophomore year of high school, and again with his brother Tony a year later.

Not that Kelli liked Mark the way she'd liked the Ballard brothers.

Before she could stop herself, she pictured the ex-bodyguard with nothing but a towel around his hips. Her face heated instantly and Lynn's eyebrow rose as if she could read Kelli's thoughts.

"Want to come help me?" Kelli asked, attention turning downward to Grace, cutting off any questions that Lynn might start throwing out.

Kelli put the dish towel over her shoulder and went to her daughter. She picked her up, and Grace giggled.

"I guess I'll go powder my nose or something," Lynn said, resigned.

"Good," Kelli said. "Less smudging on the windows before our guest gets here."

Grace started to do her routine of toddler babbling and let her mom know really quickly that she preferred to stay right where she was on her hip. So Kelli tried her best to set the table while juggling the little diva. It didn't go as well as she would have liked. Grace had become fascinated with Kelli's dangling earrings.

"Pretty," she cooed.

"Nothing compared to you." The little girl had her hair braided in pigtails and wore a long green floral shirt and pink-and-purple-striped tights she'd picked out herself. The outfit, plus her innocent smile, brightened the entire room. Kelli was so distracted by the pure love she felt for the little human that she jumped when the doorbell sounded behind them. "Our dinner guest is here."

Grace started to squirm until Kelli put her down. She ran to the door and paused to glance back at her mom. Kelli peered through the peephole to confirm it was the ex-bodyguard before giving the girl a nod. Grace squealed, and together they opened the door.

Kelli felt a single butterfly dislodge in her stomach. It began to flutter at the sight of Mark. Even though he was fully dressed, there was a new attractiveness about him now. Wearing a white button-up and a pair of nice slacks, he looked as though he'd taken pains to style his short dark hair. Though she realized his face had been shaven when she'd visited him earlier, without the presence of his half-naked body she was able to appreciate how the clean look softened his otherwise hard expression. His dark green eyes scanned her face before falling to the child at her side.

A wide smile split his face.

"You must be Grace," he said, bending to meet her gaze. She was unapologetic in her stare right back, but Kelli knew she was reverting to the rare shyness she had only when first meeting someone. Her little arms wound their way around Kelli's leg. But surprisingly, Grace smiled. "Beautiful kid," Mark added, straightening.

"And she knows it, too," Kelli responded with a wink. She moved farther back into the entryway, inviting him in.

Kelli took a quiet, quick breath when their

eyes met again. She wasn't sure what that butterfly was up to, but it was causing her to feel some things she probably shouldn't.

For a brief moment, she wondered about the love life of the man she'd just invited into her late husband's home.

Chapter Seven

Lynn managed to not lose her composure when she came into the entryway, moments after Mark shut the front door. What she didn't manage to do was keep her eyes from roving up and down the man. She cut a quick look to Kelli, who was at his side, before extending her hand.

"You must be Mark," she greeted him.

Mark took her hand. "And you must be Lynn."

The short-haired woman beamed.

"That's me—childhood best friend, keeper of all embarrassing stories, holder of everything secret. You know, the norm."

Mark chuckled, and Kelli swatted at her. Knowing her, she'd launch into one of those embarrassing stories if not adequately distracted.

"Why don't we go ahead and sit down?" she suggested, ushering the group into the next room. The table wasn't made up as fancy as she would have liked, but judging by what she had seen of his apartment, Mark didn't mind the lack of flamboyance. Like Kelli, he seemed to find pleasure in simpler tastes.

"You weren't kidding about boxes," Mark commented, taking the first seat he made it to. His back was facing the door but with a perfect sightline to a pyramid of boxes against the wall behind the table.

Kelli laughed. "I warned you."

"Yes, you did."

Lynn sat across from Mark while Grace climbed up on her lap. Normally Kelli would have said something, but the toddler had been in such a good mood that she didn't want to jeopardize it. Not that she thought Mark would have been angry if she had thrown a tantrum. He seemed to be a good man.

"I hope you like spaghetti," Kelli said, bringing in a pot full of it. "I'm not a five-star chef, but these two have never complained."

Lynn leaned in a bit but spoke loudly. "I just haven't told her that I'll never turn down free food."

Mark laughed, and the three of them launched into the small talk that happens when everyone isn't fully acquainted. Lynn brought up her disdain for her boss and, immediately after, her dream of owning her own marketing agency.

"I'd force this one here to leave her gig and get a job with me," she said, thumbing in Kelli's direction. "She can use those artsy skills to make a mean profit, helping me design pretty campaigns."

"You're still working in art therapy?" Mark

asked after downing a mouthful of noodles. Kelli was surprised he remembered.

"Actually, no," she admitted. "I currently train others to use art therapy to help senior citizens with special needs. I used to be the one *doing* it, but now I teach those who will." She shrugged. "I have to say, it's way more flexible schedule-wise, which helps me take care of that little thing there." Grace's attention was on her food, even though half of it was on her face. "Though the pay leaves room to be desired." She glanced at the boxes stacked in the living room.

"It's great what you're doing, though," Mark replied once he, too, had glanced at another stack of boxes. Kelli wondered if he'd put together the fact that her new job and its lower pay was a big contributor to them moving. "Helping people can be a hard business."

"Speaking of helping people," Lynn chimed in, "Kelli tells me you're no longer working as a bodyguard?" Kelli's eyes shot daggers at her best friend. Always one to talk before thinking, Lynn's eyes widened. She'd finally realized the most likely reason behind his change of work. However, it was too late to take her words back.

If Mark was offended, he didn't show it.

"Yeah, I needed some time away from it," he said. He didn't meet their gaze but focused on his drink. "Don't get me wrong. Orion is the best place I've ever worked, but I'd been doing it for so long, I needed a break."

Kelli hoped what he was saying was true, that he'd changed careers for reasons that didn't involve her or her family, but she certainly wasn't going to pry into his motive.

"Orion. I just love that name," Lynn said, showing Kelli she wouldn't pry, either. That earned a smile from the man.

"The founder, Nikki, named it after Orion's

belt. It was her way of remembering why she started the group."

"Why did she? What's the connection?" Kelli couldn't help but ask. Even though they'd hired Orion, she'd never heard their origin story.

"I'll warn you, it wasn't the best beginning," he said. "Nikki and I, along with two other agents, were working at an elite security agency called Redstone Solutions before Orion was even a thought. We did almost the same thing as Orion does now, but for a high price." Sadness crept across his face. Kelli realized that perhaps she'd jumped from one sore topic to another. "One day a woman named Morgan Avery came in, asking for protection while she traveled to the UK. She was competing for placement in an astronomy program that was really hard to get into. She said she'd been receiving threats and was terrified. We were told to turn her down—she didn't have enough money—but still she came day after day to ask again."

He paused. Instead of trying to find the right words, Mark looked like he was trying to forget them. "Her body was found in a ditch near the airport." Kelli and Lynn gasped. "That's when Nikki used the contacts she'd made as secretary to leave and start her own security group. She named it after Morgan's favorite constellation. She wanted to help those who couldn't afford it. Orion occasionally takes on wealthy clients to keep the place running, but the bottom line is we protect those who don't have the money for it." His frown tilted into a half smile. "And I went with her."

"Whoa," Lynn whispered.

Kelli couldn't help but agree. Warmth at the realization of why he helped people who couldn't afford it started to spread throughout her chest. Without a doubt Mark was a good man.

The conversation from there became lighter. A storm rolled in, and they found a more comfortable ground of discussing—of all things—the weather. It led to other topics mundane enough that no one was forced to remember a tragic past but interesting enough that the conversation stretched into an hour. Mark was more than the quiet man she'd met before and met once again. He livened up enough that she could see he wasn't just a bodyguard—former or otherwise—but a normal guy with a sweet smile.

He complimented her cooking and thanked her for the meal. He talked directly to Grace as much as any person could and even gave her a few compliments of her own. Lynn must have decided she liked him, as well. Without asking Kelli or Mark, she cleared the table and replaced their dishes with wineglasses.

"It's storming outside, so it's not like you can leave right now," she explained to Mark.

"While we wait, let's have a glass of this wine I was polite enough to bring over."

Kelli found that she quite liked that idea.

"You said you'll never turn down free food?" Mark asked Lynn, eyeing the bottle. "I won't turn down free wine."

THE STORM DIDN'T DISSIPATE.

The longer they waited, the worse it got. If Grace hadn't skipped her nap, she would have been terrified. As it was, she was bundled up in Kelli's bed, fast asleep. But with the growing volume of each boom of thunder, she wouldn't be for long.

It was well past ten and Lynn, Mark and Kelli had thoroughly exhausted all small talk. A majority of *that* had been done by the vivacious best friend who hadn't been shy with the wine she'd brought over. Whether she was making sure to fill the conversational void constantly or was just really excited for new company, Kelli couldn't tell. What she did know was that Mark had been nothing but polite. He hadn't been quiet, but she realized he hadn't said much about himself, either. The only time he'd momentarily opened up was about Orion before the wine. Past that? It was like talking to a ghost.

It made her wonder how he lived his life.

And how much of it he didn't.

"If you think I'm letting you two leave in this—" Kelli motioned to the living room's front windows "—then you're sadly mistaken."

Mark's head was tilted down over his phone, but he chuckled. "It isn't that bad," he said.

Lynn, who had taken up the other side of the couch, moved her head to see what he was looking at. "That's a very red radar," she commented.

Mark sighed. "Yes, it is."

Kelli stood from the chair opposite them

and put her hands together. "Then it looks like we're all bunking here tonight."

Mark's eyebrow shot up so fast that Kelli instantly questioned her decision.

"Listen, you took a taxi here right?" she asked. He nodded.

"I realized my truck was running on empty," he admitted. "I thought it would be easier to just grab a cab here instead."

"Well, they aren't going to send someone out in this, and even if they did, would you trust them to get you home all right?" On cue, the sound of rain pelting the house intensified. She could tell the man was now reaching the same conclusion. "If you don't mind taking the couch, Lynn, you can bunk with me and the munchkin since her room is all packed up. Okay?"

Lynn reached over and patted Mark on the shoulder before standing with her empty wineglass.

"Don't fight it, man," she said. "That look

she's sporting? That's her Mama Bear face. Right now she doesn't see us as people. We're her cubs." Mark laughed.

"Call it a side effect of motherhood," Kelli responded, hands going to her hips. She fixed Mark with a less intense stare. "I can't make you stay, but I assure you it's no inconvenience to us."

Mark glanced at the window and the dark abyss outside. He was hesitant in answering. "If it's really no trouble, then it might be a good idea to stay, at least till it passes."

Kelli smiled and Lynn clapped. The sound was drowned out by another *boom* of thunder. It didn't diminish her cheer.

"Haven't had a sleepover in years," she squealed.

Kelli promptly rolled her eyes.

THE DAY HAD been full of surprises, but now the night was trumping them. Mark settled back onto the couch, trying to get comfortable under the multicolored blanket. Kelli had said Victor had never been a fan of its brightness. Bringing Victor up, however relevant he was, had put a feeling of guilt and confusion within him once again.

Now the house was as quiet as the storm outside would let it be. The light kept on in the kitchen buzzed through the madness. Neither of these things kept Mark awake. It was the room across from him that grabbed his focus and kept it.

Victor Crane's office.

Kelli had mentioned it was the last room they had packed and as soon as she'd said it, her expression had darkened. That's where she'd found the notebook.

Mark let out a long breath and tried to readjust to a more comfortable position. Nothing was working. His mind was refusing to shut down for the night. After a few more minutes of no success, he pulled out his phone and checked the radar again.

"Desperate to leave?"

Mark sat up quickly, turning toward the hallway that separated the living room and kitchen. In the dim light, Kelli smiled.

"Sorry, I didn't mean to startle you," she apologized. "Unlike the two ladies passed out in my bed, I can't sleep through all of this."

"And here I thought I was the only one," he responded. His voice had dropped in volume to match hers, but every part of him had to focus to keep it from getting too deep. As she stood there in a tank top and plaid boxers, with no makeup, her short hair in a ponytail, Mark found himself admiring how beautiful she was.

"Well, since we can't seem to fall asleep, would you be interested in a late-night snack?" She grinned. "I know where Grace's mom hides the chocolate-chip cookies."

For the umpteenth time that night, Kelli made

him laugh. It was not only a foreign feeling to him but also a sound he wasn't used to hearing.

"As long as you don't tell, I won't," he responded with a wink. Kelli's smile grew, and Mark followed her into the kitchen. Wanting to avoid another shirtless session with her, he'd been mindful to keep his undershirt on when he had first lain down.

The light above the sink was enough to illuminate the room. It showed Kelli climbing up onto the countertop next to the refrigerator. She looked back at his questioning look before opening up the small cabinet above.

"You really made sure Grace couldn't reach those, huh?" he whispered.

She laughed softly. "And Lynn." Kelli found the bag of cookies and passed it back to him. "Keeping any sweets in the house has proven to be a very difficult thing to—"

Another *boom* of thunder hit, but the sound that immediately followed wasn't storm-related at all. It was glass shattering. Both of them turned their heads toward the living room, even though the wall was in their way. Frozen, they listened.

Another crash was partially masked by the storm.

Every part of Mark went on high alert. He crept along the kitchen wall until he was at the doorway. Crouching so he wasn't at full height, he looked across the hallway to the room he had just been trying to sleep in. Past the couch and through the double French doors, movement caught his eye.

Someone was climbing through the office window. Judging by the flashlight in his hand and the mask on his face, it wasn't a person filled with good intentions.

Mark moved quickly back to Kelli. His face must have shown it all. She didn't question when he grabbed her by the waist. She put her hands on his shoulders, and he lifted her up off the countertop and set her back down on the floor. He took her hand and pulled her through the other kitchen doorway that opened farther down the hallway. The intruder couldn't see them as Mark rushed them to the master bedroom. But that also meant they couldn't see the intruder.

Once they were in the bedroom, Mark turned and quietly shut the door behind them. He threw the lock before turning to his hostess. The nightstand lamp illuminated her face. Acute worry shone clearly across it—so intense it almost gave him pause.

Almost.

"A man in a mask just broke into the office. I can't tell if he was armed," he whispered, taking his cell phone out of his pocket. He handed it to her and went to the bed where Grace and Lynn were fast asleep. He shook the woman. It took her a second, but her eyes finally fluttered open. He put a finger to his lips when she opened her mouth. "Take Grace into the bathroom and lock the door." Surprisingly, Lynn didn't argue. Without comment, she scurried out of bed.

Mark went back to Kelli, who was whispering into the phone. She watched with wide eyes as her best friend carried her still-sleeping daughter into the en suite. It was those wide eyes that he was looking into when the lamp and the bathroom light cut off. He could hear the dying whirl of the ceiling fan as it powered down.

He cursed beneath his breath before a hand reached out and took his.

"Either the storm or the intruder just cut the power," Kelli whispered to the 911 operator. Whatever the operator said back to her, he didn't hear. She squeezed his hand, pulling him closer. Suddenly her breath was next to his ear. "There's a flashlight under the bathroom sink."

122 Full Force Fatherhood

It was Kelli's turn to pull him along. He didn't stop her. She knew the house better.

"Lynn, take the phone," Kelli whispered when they were inside the bathroom. There was noise, and then Lynn was the one whispering to the operator. The glow of the phone illuminated her sitting in the soaker tub, Grace asleep still in her arms.

Kelli didn't drop Mark's hand as she retrieved a giant flashlight from beneath the counter. She clicked it on. He was surprised to see that the worry she had exuded earlier had changed into something else. He couldn't place it and didn't have time to. She turned to her best friend.

"Stay here and don't open this door. And keep Grace safe no matter what," she ground out, turning the lock inside the door before shutting it and taking Mark with her into the bedroom. No hesitation lined her movements.

"There's a gun in the nightstand," she whispered, hurrying over to retrieve it. "But it doesn't have a clip." Her face fell. "I separated them just in case Grace found it…and I've already packed it up." Mark scanned the boxes that lined the wall.

"They don't know that," he said, taking the black 9 mm. It was undoubtedly empty, weighing significantly less than when it was loaded. He held the grip with one hand. With the other, he cupped the bottom, where the clip would normally be. If he kept it there, no one would be the wiser.

Until he needed to shoot it.

"What are you going to do?" Kelli kept the flashlight's beam on the floor. The beam bounced off the hardwood to give them just enough lighting to see the shadows on each other's faces.

"I'm going to go greet our new guest."

"But can't we just wait for the police?"

The storm kept its loud pace outside.

"I'm not confident in their response time,"

he said, already moving Kelli back to the bathroom door. "Stay and turn the light off."

"Be careful," she whispered.

The flashlight cut off. He waited a moment for his eyes to readjust to the darkness before creeping back into the hallway. The storm wasn't helping him hear exactly where the intruder was, but by the same token, the intruder probably didn't hear him, either. It helped he was barefoot.

Slowly he followed the cool hardwood back toward the living room. Without the kitchen light on, the house was bathed in darkness. The occasional lightning flash lit up his surroundings.

He mentally pulled up the layout of the house, thanks to a quick tour Kelli had given him after supper. The only way to get to the women was to go through him or the bedroom window. He doubted the intruder would go back outside just to break back in. If he did, he knew Kelli would let him know.

Mark slowed at the arch that opened into the living room. He heard rustling but couldn't tell where exactly it was coming from. Pulling the gun up as if it were actually loaded, he swung around into the room. Judging by the size and form, the intruder was a man. Broad shoulders couldn't be hidden by the black jacket he wore. He was no longer in the office but by a stack of boxes behind the couch in the living room. Mark had hoped to be quiet enough to surprise him completely, but the man turned at his presence.

Mark immediately noted the gloves and ski mask he wore.

And the knife in his hand. Even from a distance in the low light, he could see it was at least six inches in length.

"Drop the knife and put your hands up," Mark barked, making sure to keep his hand firm over the empty space where the clip should have been. He tried quickly to discern any details that might give him an edge over the mystery man if things went south. The intruder wasn't as big as Mark, but that didn't mean he didn't know how to fight. The flashlight he'd had when Mark had first seen him was set on the back of the couch. It partially lit up the room but not enough to piece together the intruder's expression or intention beneath his mask. "I said, *drop it*," Mark repeated, moving closer. He wanted to show the man he wasn't joking.

"And here I thought the ladies were alone." The way the man said it put Mark further on edge. There was no worry or remorse in his words. Almost as if he was stating a lazy fact.

"Drop the knife or I'll drop you." Mark lowered his voice to a level he hoped was pure threat. The man wasn't showing any signs of fear. He moved the knife to his other hand.

"'Drop me,' eh? Been watching a lot of cop shows, haven't you?"

"Can't say I'm the only one," Mark bit out. "Looks like you've been taking pointers from some lowlifes. I'd rather be the cop than the thief."

The man chuckled.

"I may be stealing something, but I'm no thief," he responded, starting to move slowly around the couch. Mark was surprised he was coming closer rather than trying to flee. He had no way of knowing there was no clip inside the gun. "But I don't have to explain myself to you."

Later Mark would be able to look back and realize that the small smile that brought up the corner of the man's lips right after he spoke was the exact moment he knew that the man was dangerous. That, without a doubt, the intruder was an immediate threat not only to Mark but also to the women in the house.

But in the moment, he felt his body act of its own accord.

He threw the gun at the man with all the strength he had. Clearly surprised, the intruder didn't duck out of the way. The gun hit his shoulder hard. The knife in his hand clattered to the ground.

Mark didn't hesitate.

Chapter Eight

The two men hit the far wall with enough force that Mark heard the man's breath push out. Mark wanted to get the man away from his weapon and subdue him. Tackling him into a wall seemed to be the best of both worlds.

However, it was Mark's turn to be surprised. The man might have lost his breath, but he hadn't lost his fighting skills. He brought up his fist and gave Mark a good right hook. Pain burst behind his eye just as the man brought his foot right on top of Mark's instep. The combination made him waver enough that the intruder was able to push Mark backward into the couch.

"Is that it, bodyguard?"

How had he known Mark was a bodyguard? Ex or otherwise?

Mark balled his fists and brought his feet apart just in time for the intruder to lunge forward.

He swung high. Mark ducked low.

They went through another flurry of fists before the man threw a punch that landed so close to Mark's face that he lost his balance trying to dodge it. The intruder used the gap in defense to his advantage. He threw his shoulder into Mark's chest, and together they toppled over the couch.

Mark's head hit the coffee table, dazing him. The intruder pushed off him and made a run for his knife, lying a few feet from them.

"I don't think so," Mark hissed, scrambling to grab the man. He wasn't fast enough. The man picked up his weapon. He turned so fast that Mark froze.

"I'm no thief, but I don't mind fighting," the man said, brandishing the too-large knife.

Mark was so close that if the man jumped forward, he'd slice him with ease. Images of the three ladies in the bedroom flashed behind his eyes. He needed to get that knife away from the man, no matter what.

Just as he was gearing up to grab the man's wrist, something small flew over his shoulder. It hit the intruder's nose. He yelled in pain. Mark used the opening to grab the man's wrist and bend it backward. The knife once again dropped to the ground. Mark didn't waste time in retrieving it.

"Don't move," Mark ground out, knife in hand. The man's eyes—dark, Mark couldn't tell what color—darted from the weapon to a space over Mark's shoulder. Without another comment, he turned and ran back into the office. Mark tried to catch him but the man was fast.

He jumped through the window he'd broken and disappeared into the stormy night.

Mark wanted to follow him—to catch him—but a sound behind him drew his attention away.

Kelli stood in the living room doorway, eyes wide.

"I found the clip," she said, voice a few octaves too high. Mark didn't understand until he followed her gaze to the floor near the couch. Despite the situation, he let out a loud laugh.

"That's what hit him," he realized. "You *threw* the clip at him."

Kelli shrugged.

"I panicked," she admitted. "I thought he was going to stab you. I can't believe it actually hit him. I can barely see."

"We're quite the couple, then." Mark walked over to the discarded gun, partially under the couch thanks to the scuffle, and retrieved its clip. Working at Orion had trained him to shy away from using guns—there were other ways to disable an attacker—but he wasn't about to just leave it on the floor, either. He put the safety on and secured the gun in the back of his pants. "I threw the gun at him when I realized he wasn't going to give up."

Kelli let out her own little laugh, but it didn't last long.

Mark sobered. "The cops are on their way?"

"Yeah, the dispatcher said it might take a little bit because of the storm." Kelli took a few steps forward and extended her hand to him. Unsure of what to do, he took it. The light from the flashlight made shadows dance across her concerned face. The nerves boiling beneath his skin began to die down.

They were safe.

Kelli was safe.

"Are you okay?" she asked, not fazed by

their contact. Mark wondered how well she could read him. Surprise at her thoughtfulness toward him was all he could feel for a moment. His slow response time only seemed to heighten that concern. "*Did* he cut you?"

"No, I'm fine. All he got in were a few punches." Pain in his head started to rise in his awareness. He glanced over to the coffee table. "But I think I might have cracked your coffee table."

Kelli didn't even turn to look. She squeezed his hand. "Thank you," she whispered.

He squeezed back. "Thank *you*. I have no doubt that he would have used this." Mark dropped her hand and held the knife up.

"Do you think his fingerprints are still on it?"

Mark shook his head, recalling the gloves the intruder had worn. "He came prepared."

Kelli grabbed the flashlight and pointed it to the office. Mark watched as she moved the beam across the now-open boxes from a safe distance.

"That's my laptop," she said, pausing in her movement. "I almost never use it. It's basically brand-new." She moved the light back into the living room to the open box that obviously held the stereo. "It's not a brand-new model, but it's worth money." The light moved again until it rested between them, showing him the clear expression of someone who has just discovered something they wish they hadn't. "Mark, I don't know why, but I think he was looking for Victor's journal."

Mark thought back to the purse snatching. The mugger had left the purse…and nothing had been taken. Now, in the dead of night, in the middle of a storm, a man decked out in black had broken in. What's more, he'd admitted he was no thief but was after *something*.

That was too many coincidences.

Sirens sounded in the distance. Mark met Kelli's gaze with certainty.

"I think I'm officially on the paranoid train."

THE POLICE BROUGHT in rain and mud and a lot of questions. Kelli, ready to deal with all three, was immensely thankful that Mark was more than willing to walk the cops through everything that had happened. Not leaving any details out. So when he got to the part about her throwing the clip at the intruder's head—an act of sheer panic on her part—the two men paused and looked her way.

Grace, now fully awake on Kelli's hip, waved at them. Mark was the only one who did a little wave back before taking the officers through the rest of the story. He stepped with them over to the broken office window, and together all three stood with heads tilted.

"This sleepover was almost as bad as Marcie

Diggle's fifteenth birthday party," Lynn said from the dining table's chair behind her.

"Just because you found out Marcie kissed Tim Duncan," she replied.

Lynn snapped her fingers.

"Yeah, a week after he kissed *me*." She crossed her arms over her chest. The pajama set she'd borrowed had already been switched back to her earlier clothes. Kelli knew the way old friends do that Lynn was using humor to stay calm. She turned away from the men and patted Lynn's shoulder.

"You did good, Lynn," she said, tone void of any playful tease. "We're lucky to have you in our lives."

The dark-haired woman's expression softened. A small smile brought up the corners of her lips. She touched Kelli's hand.

"We're also lucky the storm kept Mark here." She glanced over to the ex-bodyguard. "He kept calm, really calm."

Kelli nodded at that. "It used to be his job."

"I guess it was good timing you invited him for dinner. Though maybe next time you invite him somewhere, you should go ahead and invite the cops, too."

Kelli wanted to tell Lynn right then that she believed the mugging and the break-in were a result of Victor's work, but at the same time she knew she wouldn't tell her. Lynn had been her confidant since before puberty. Apart from Grace, there was no one she loved more in the world. Telling Lynn that she might have stumbled across a conspiracy that had gotten her husband killed was getting the woman too close to danger. Lynn hurt—or worse—was an unimaginable danger she wanted to avoid at all costs.

Right then and there, Kelli made up her mind to keep Lynn in the dark.

"Kelli?" Mark called after the officers went back to their car to retrieve their camera. The ex-bodyguard, still shoeless and in his under-shirt, met her in the middle of the living room with a face filled with concentration. Grace put her cheek back on her mother's shoulder but turned her head to watch the man speak. She was always curious. "They said they're going to take some pictures for evidence and finish taking both of our statements. They put out an APB for the man and have a patrol car look-ing, but if that guy is half as smart as I think he is, he'll have used the weather to hide." Mark paused, giving a quick smile to the little girl before sobering again. "That being said, I think it might be best if you don't stay here tonight."

"Oh, don't worry, we won't," she agreed. "Lynn already offered us her guest bedroom. Though…" Kelli placed her hand on Grace's back and began to rub it, the motion soothing her probably more than the girl. "I wasn't at home last night when I was mugged, Mark. What if we're right and someone is after the journal? What if they keep coming after me—after us—until they find it? Being across the city won't make a difference. We'll still be in danger."

It was a dark thought but also a real possibility. Keeping her family safe was all that mattered, and now she wasn't sure how to keep doing it.

Mark didn't immediately respond. His dark eyes were trying to have a conversation with her that she couldn't exactly understand. One that drew his brow together and thinned his lips before he finally spoke.

"Then we'll have to figure out who is after it and why," he decided. The decisive *we* he inserted filled her with an odd excitement. As well as relief. Sharing the burden of fear—no matter the degree of selfishness—made the situation less terrifying.

"But what about until we do?" She paused

her rubbing motion on Grace's back. "How do we stay safe?"

"I know someone who might help with that."

MARK MOVED THIS way and that—trying to get comfortable. The front seat didn't give. He let out a long exhalation. Instead of trying a new position, he let his body become still again. The street outside Lynn's town house was quiet after the storm. He sat in Kelli's car. Lynn's neighbors paid Mark no mind if they saw him, which he doubted.

He'd been sitting there since he'd driven the tired women over. After the police had left and they'd put up a makeshift tarp over Kelli's broken window, Kelli had pulled him aside to let him know just how much she didn't want to involve Lynn. Not until they had concrete proof.

"I want to keep her safe, and isn't ignorance bliss?" she had said with fake humor. It had disappeared quickly. *"Plus, she's taken on a lot*

with Grace and me since Victor's death. I—I have to be certain before I drag her in."

Mark saw the reason in her desire to keep her best friend in the dark. If he could, he'd keep Kelli out of the loop, too. But whoever was after the journal certainly hadn't thought twice about making contact with her. The fact that the man had known the house was filled with the young family and Lynn, and had come in armed anyway was something that made his blood boil.

The Cranes had already been through enough.

Mark rolled his shoulders back and stifled a yawn. His eyes fell to the journal on his lap. Kelli had offered the evidence to him so she wouldn't be alone in knowing what Victor had once known, too. It was strange to read the man's notes in a way. Seeing the words he had written and knowing that the journalist knew nothing of his tragic fate made the guilt in

Mark rise to the surface. If only he could have stopped the man in black…

Just as another yawn was making its way through Mark, the front door of Lynn's town house opened. Kelli, dressed in a blue T-shirt from the Dallas Zoo and jeans, walked out with two cups in her hands. Her short hair hung darker, wet from an apparent shower, but she clearly had makeup on. A messenger bag was slung across her chest. The closer she came, the more he realized he was drinking in all of her details. Shifting in his seat, as if that could ease the sudden guilt, he unlocked the passenger door and pasted on a smile.

"I'm going to assume you're tired," Kelli greeted him, not pausing as she got in the car. "I'm also going to assume you're a fan of coffee with a lot of sugar." She handed the cup over, and he laughed.

"I'm not one to turn down free sugary coffee."

Kelli smiled, pleased.

"Nothing out of the ordinary here?" she swiveled her head around to see both directions of the street. He already knew what it looked like. The scenery would change when people began to leave for work.

"Thankfully it's been pretty quiet."

"How do you not lose your mind sitting here for hours with nothing happening? Let alone stay awake?" Kelli's eyebrows pinched in question. It was something he'd been asked countless times while on the job with Orion.

"Years of experience, I guess." He held up the journal as an example of some of what he'd done and passed it to her. She silently placed it in her purse, but Mark could see she wanted more, so he brought up another man from his past. "A friend I worked with at Orion, Oliver, used to tell me the key to keeping focused and sharp—no matter where or what case you were working—was to keep rescanning your environment over and over again as if it was the first time you'd seen it. Because, and I quote, 'It's the little things that change and bite you in the ass.'" He smiled. "Pardon my French, but that's pretty much how I've worked for years. Making sure none of the details go unnoticed can keep a person busy, even if nothing changes." Mark couldn't help but think about the night at the cabin. He'd done the same thing both inside and outside the cabin, and yet...

"Details. I'm not so good at those," Kelli said, taking a big sip of coffee. "I think having a toddler has fried my brain."

"She's pretty cool. Grace, that is." Mark motioned to the house. "She seems like a sharp kid for her age."

"Thanks. I think so, too."

A different kind of smile wound up the corners of the woman's lips. Pride mixed with unmistakable love. Guilt for not being able to protect the father of the family was replaced by an ache of loneliness within him. It caught him off guard. He didn't like it.

"So, what's on the docket for the day?" Mark changed the subject but was annoyed that the feeling stayed.

"Lynn is watching Grace—because she's a wonderful person—while I go to talk to Dennis Crawford. I told her we were tying up some break-in loose ends."

Mark's eyebrow rose. "That name sounds familiar," he said.

Kelli's expression hardened behind her coffee cup.

"He was Victor's editor for the Bowman Foundation spotlight," she explained. "He's also the only person other than you whom I've brought up my concerns to. And since I'm pretty certain you weren't the person who mugged me and then broke into my house..."

"You think he knows something," Mark finished.

"Or is our culprit."

"So you're going to go and—what—confront the man you think is behind it all?" Even as he asked, he realized that was exactly what Kelli intended to do. "Kelli, if this guy *is* behind this whole thing, then going to see him is dangerous."

Kelli fixed him with a pointed stare. "Good thing I have a bodyguard, then."

Her comment was playful, but it created a storm of emotions inside him. As with his comment about her daughter being smart, he felt an ounce of pride, a measure of pleasure and the ever-present blanket of guilt beneath both. Without knowing what he was about to say, he was glad he didn't have to respond right away. A car pulled up in front of them. It drew Kelli's attention away from him.

"Speaking of bodyguards."

Chapter Nine

Jonathan Carmichael didn't look like a bodyguard at first glance. Although he was muscled
and had an unmistakable set to his jaw that
spoke of discipline and determination, he was
leaner and taller than his original teammates,
Mark and Oliver. From personal experience,
Mark knew that even though the black-haired
man looked slight next to him, his physical appearance didn't diminish the man's abilities. He
was the rock of their once-close group. Always
sensible, always strong.

Jonathan Carmichael was the guy who surprised everyone.

Seeing him cut his engine and get out of the car, waiting for Mark to make his way over, was definitely something Mark hadn't realized he missed. In a way it felt as though they were getting ready for a job—though he supposed that was kind of what they *were* doing.

"Long time, no see," Jonathan greeted him. He extended his hand and they shook. "I see your scruff has gotten better." He motioned to Mark's chin and his five-o'clock shadow. It made Mark laugh.

"I actually shaved yesterday. I was trying to do you proud," he joked back. Mark had wondered what their first meeting since the last time he'd seen him—at least six months ago—would be like. He was glad Jonathan seemed to be there with humor rather than anger. The past was more than creeping up on Mark. He couldn't take another problem to think about. "Thanks for coming on such short notice and with little to no explanation."

Jonathan shrugged, glancing at Kelli, who was still sitting in the car.

"We may not be hanging out like we used to, but I can still tell when you're spooked."

"I can't deny that this whole thing is…unsettling." It was his turn to look back at Kelli. "And that one is a firecracker. She won't back down, and I—well, I need to keep her and her family safe, and I can't do that by myself right now."

Jonathan, the middle ground between Oliver's compassion and Mark's normally stoic reasoning, nodded, while a twitch of his lips pulled up at the corner, moving his impeccable goatee.

"Well, I'm happy to help. But—" Jonathan lowered his voice, not to show he was trying to be secretive but instead to convey seriousness "—I'm able to be here because Nikki moved a contract around. She didn't question me getting out of work, but she expects an answer why. And we both know she deserves one."

Mark knew as soon as he'd called Jonathan the night before that eventually he'd have to talk with Nikki again. Still he sighed.

"I know," he admitted.

"Good. Now, tell *me* what's going on."

KELLI WAS TRYING not to pout. She was almost thirty, for goodness' sake, yet there she was, riding shotgun to the Orion Security Group, trying her best not to show she was ribbed about not getting to go confront the potential culprit. Mark was quiet—ignoring the fact that she was upset she hadn't gotten her way.

"I remember him—Jonathan—from when I first came into Orion," she said when she could no longer stand the quiet. "His résumé was impressive, and if I remember correctly, he was one of the original Orion agents? Like you?"

Mark gave a half smile. There was no doubt

in Kelli's mind that he'd been hiding his emotions since they'd reconnected—maybe a trade secret of the security business—but she could see his feelings for his friend were genuine.

"Yes, Jonathan and I were a part of the first team at Orion. Along with Oliver Quinn."

"The man who helped the private investigator catch a killer in Maine," she supplied. "That's how we heard of Orion in the first place. It was all over the news."

Mark chuckled. "Fun fact—that private investigator is now his wife."

"Really?"

"They were childhood sweethearts who reconnected after a long time. He now runs the freelance division of Orion, dealing with specialists and strategists who might be needed."

"What about his wife? Is she still a private investigator?"

Mark nodded. "Oh, yeah, you couldn't get her to stop if you begged. But Oliver never did.

And between you and me, I think they help each other on their respective cases."

"Sounds like you're in with a well-connected crowd."

Mark's smile wavered.

"I was. Orion wasn't the only thing I distanced myself from when I quit." His jaw hardened as he said it. His eyes stayed on the road ahead. Kelli wanted to pry—to understand the motive behind him leaving—but she felt she already knew the reason. Mark had done so much for her in the past two days that she decided not to make him open old wounds.

Victor's death had changed more than just her life.

ORION SECURITY GROUP'S main office looked more or less the same as it had all those years ago when it had first opened. A modest one-story standalone wrapped in brick and beige siding, Orion's name was painted in large white letters above the door that, as Nikki had said, made it feel as if Orion was watching over you as you entered the business. As they walked inside, Mark eyed these letters with nostalgia.

The lobby, like the building, was modest in size and decoration. A young Hispanic woman named Jillian sat behind a desk that broke up the space between the front door and the rest of the office. She acted as its part-time guard and had been there for almost three years. When she saw them, her already fifteen-hundred-watt smile brightened.

"Mark!" Within the space of a heartbeat, Jillian was around her desk and hugging him. Kelli raised her eyebrow but was soon enveloped in a hug of her own. "Hello, Mrs. Crane!" Mark shared a look over the girl's head that he hoped said, "I'll explain later."

Jillian backed off.

"Nikki told me you were coming in," she said, still all smiles. "It's been a long time since

I've seen either of you." Her eyes flitted over Kelli. "I sent some flowers but I never got to tell you—in person—sorry for your loss of Victor."

Kelli didn't skip a beat. "Thank you."

Jillian turned back to Mark, somberness gone. "I'm glad you're back. It hasn't been the same around here without you."

"Thanks, but don't get used to this. I'm just here to talk with the boss."

She gave a small nod and threw her thumb over her shoulder. "She's all yours, but I'll warn you, she hasn't had her coffee yet."

Mark let out a breath. Just what he needed. A Nikki without her heavenly coffee.

"Who was that?" Kelli whispered. They were walking past Oliver Quinn's old office and Jonathan's current empty one. Mark's, or what used to be his, was opposite. Though Orion had expanded and no longer operated solely within teams, team leads still had their own offices. Even if they weren't around long enough to use them.

"Right before Orion first started its expansion, Jillian showed up asking if we had an internship program," he explained. "We didn't, but she made a compelling case. Now she's the part-time secretary while she takes college cybersecurity classes. She's a nice girl—tough as nails."

Kelli looked over her shoulder. A smile turned up her lips. "I can see why Nikki likes her, then."

They made it past the open area between the break room and the workout room—what Jonathan had once likened to the grazing field where agents would spend their downtime hanging out on the couches or watching sports on the wall-mounted TV—right up to the last office in the building. It was large, with three of its walls made of glass. Nikki's dark red hair could be seen bobbing behind the computer screen on the desk in the middle of the room.

"Should I wait out here? Or—" Kelli motioned to the couches behind them. Instead of looking as if she was afraid of the often intimidating Nikki Waters, Kelli merely seemed to be respectful of their privacy. But if he was ever going to sell his former boss on the theory that Victor's piece on a charity had gotten him killed, he needed the widow to back him up.

"If you don't mind, I think we should both tell her what's going on."

Kelli lowered her voice, even though Jillian and Nikki were the only other people they'd seen in the entire building.

"Do you think it's a good idea to tell someone else? We've already told Jonathan."

Mark had thought it over during the car ride.

"Keeping Nikki in the dark would be much harder to do since we're using Jonathan for help. She'd give us more trouble than we need right now. Plus, she can be one hell of an ally."

"All right," Kelli concluded. "I trust you."

Guilt exploded within his chest. Those three little words stabbed at his heart. Probing the spot that reminded him Victor Crane had also trusted him. He adjusted his smile—sure that it had sagged—and knocked on the door.

"Come in," his former boss called.

Mark took a deep breath, and together they went inside.

NIKKI'S HAIR WAS longer than when Kelli had first met her years ago, but she still had kind eyes, only hardening when needed. She came around the desk with her hand outstretched.

"Nice to see you again, Kelli," she said. Her grip was gentle yet firm. Nikki waved them to the seats opposite her.

"I'm glad you've come by," she started, bypassing any small talk. "To say I'm curious why you two are hanging out is an understatement."

Mark shifted in his seat. Kelli wondered if he was worried about whether Nikki would believe their story or just about her reaction to it. The woman who had gone from secretary to founder and boss of a successful—and moral—security group had to be tough.

How tough, Kelli was about to find out.

Mark straightened his back and dove right in. He rehashed his belief that Darwin hadn't set the fire and explained why they thought the mugging, the break-in and Dennis Crawford were all somehow connected.

"That's why I wanted to ask to have a check done on him," Mark said. "He knows something that could help us figure out what's going on."

Nikki threaded her fingers together over the desktop. "You have no evidence whatsoever that ties Dennis to the fire. You have a theory, one that's loose, and built *and* propelled by grief." She shared a look between them before stopping on Kelli. "I am truly sorry for your loss, and can't imagine what you have had to go through. I'm also sorry that the past few days have been less than great."

She turned back to Mark. "You spent a solid year looking for your man in black. During that year you quit your job, quit your friends and came up with what? Nothing but a box filled with files that lead you to nowhere but self-isolation. I'm sorry, but I won't help you go back to that world, if only for the basic reason that you no longer work at Orion and will not receive its benefits." In one fluid movement, Nikki stood and moved to the office door. She held it open. "There is such a thing as coincidences and bad luck and timing, and I think that's all it is."

Kelli didn't need look at Mark to know that the conversation was through. They would not be getting Nikki's help. They would not be granted a reprieve. She followed the man out with only a nod to Nikki as they passed.

Jillian didn't stop them as they left through the lobby, and Mark didn't even say goodbye. Kelli couldn't tell if he was mad, disappointed or embarrassed. Whatever he was feeling, he was definitely silent as they drove away.

It was a silence that Kelli couldn't take for long.

"So, Nikki mentioned you had a box of files on the fire that killed Victor?"

Mark took in a long breath before letting it go out in a whoosh.

"Yes. Everything I collected in the year after." He lowered his voice as if he was being scolded for a mistake. "I was looking for something—*anything*—that could help me—" he paused "—understand." Kelli knew the look of guilt he was trying to hide. It was one she was starting to feel when looking at Mark. Not because he couldn't save Victor, but because of what she realized she was starting to feel for the ex-bodyguard. Instead of trying to sort her thoughts out on the future, she tried to focus on the present.

"I'd like to see that box, if you don't mind."

"Really?"

"Yes. Let's figure out why Darwin McGregor lied."

MARK DISAPPEARED INTO his bedroom for a few minutes. He wouldn't tell her where the box of files was, but she had a sneaking suspicion it was well hidden.

Kelli took the time to check in on Lynn and Grace. Both were watching cartoons in their pajamas. One reason why Lynn made such a great babysitter was that she was a grown-up child herself. Sometimes Grace had to let her know when *she* was done playing.

Lynn thankfully didn't ask too many questions. Kelli let the woman keep thinking she was dealing with the break-in and house issues for the day. Which wasn't too far from the truth. Finding out who wanted the journal was intrinsically tied to the break-in.

"Sorry," Mark said, breaking the silence. "I was a little too nondescript when labeling this. Not to mention I think I might have tried to hide it from myself." He put a box on the coffee table and took the seat next to her on the couch.

"I see what you meant about being nondescript," she commented. The box was devoid of any telling signs of what might be inside. It was an utterly ordinary brown with the top taped down. He pulled a pocketknife from his jeans but set it on the table.

"Are you sure you want to see all of this?" he asked, keeping his gaze on the box. "To say this isn't filled with bad memories would be a lie."

For one long moment, Kelli considered his words. She had been excited at the idea that Mark had files that could lead them to who was behind Victor's death and attempting to steal his journal. Yet it wasn't until that moment that she realized the past was neatly packed up a few inches from her. Was she ready to face tangible proof of the past instead of the memories that still haunted her at any mention or sight of smoke?

"No, I need to do this," she decided. "If not to find justice for Victor, then to ensure Grace's safety."

"Then, here we go."

Chapter Ten

"So give me *your* summary on all of this." Kelli waved her hand over the papers and pictures on the coffee table. They had spent the past half hour in silence, each combing through what Mark had collected. Most notable were the copies of the police report on Darwin McGregor, the rough sketch Mark had drawn of the man he claimed was responsible, and Orion's origin file on Victor and Kelli. She'd only glanced at that last one, pushing it to the side to look at later.

Mark ran his hand across the stubble on his chin and put down the pictures in his hand.

They were of Victor's family cabin the day after the fire. She'd already glanced at those, too, but decided to keep her distance. On her darkest days, she could sometimes close her eyes and see the flames devouring the structure during the dead of night.

"On the surface it's simple," he started. "A dumb kid who likes starting fires sets fire to a cabin. In the process he blows up the propane tank. Which sets off a chain reaction that eventually destroys the entire place…and a man is killed because of it." He didn't pause, and Kelli was grateful for it. "He confesses in court that he intended to set the fire and—bonus—it's not his first one, so he's tried as an adult and sent to prison. Then everyone forgets about it. Well, you know what I mean."

He put his hand on the paper closest to him— the sketch of the man. "But I saw a man in black, bigger than the boy, spreading the fire. A man no one else thought existed." His eyes rounded a fraction. "A man I now realize bears a striking resemblance to the man who broke into your house last night." Kelli tried to interrupt, but Mark continued. "He set the fire, *intending* to have no survivors, and then disappeared. Darwin wasn't caught until the next morning, miles away from the cabin. Do you remember how he acted in court?"

Kelli didn't have to think hard. "Crude."

Mark nodded. "He certainly wasn't trying to sell that he was sorry for what he'd done. Even with his grandmother looking on the entire time."

Kelli remembered the young man's lack of empathy as he recounted setting the fires, later answering without pause that it wasn't the first time. He hadn't shown an ounce of regret despite claiming that he knew exactly what his actions had cost Kelli and her unborn child.

She cleared her throat. "I remember hearing her cry," she said. The sound of the older woman crying had created a background noise that had competed with Kelli's own sobs. Before Grace had been born, she hadn't always been rock solid. Then again, no one had expected her to be.

"She raised Darwin," Mark said. "I think he was the only family she had. I looked her up out of curiosity a few months after the trial. She's holed up in some lakeside retirement home."

That caught Kelli's attention.

"Lakeside retirement home?" she asked, pulling out her phone. "Do you know the name of it, by chance?"

"Uh, something about an apple? I can't remember, but I know it's just outside Wilmington, North Carolina. Darwin was a local there." Kelli pulled up the search browser on her phone. "Why?"

She put up a finger to tell him to wait. Her heartbeat started to speed up. Close to a clue?

Reaching? She didn't know which was more accurate. But when she found what she was looking for she made a noise that was caught between an *aha* and a gasp.

"Appleton Retreat," she said, handing her phone over. The website for the retirement home was pulled up. Its gallery of photos were on a slideshow on the homepage.

"Okay…what am I looking at, exactly?"

"Darwin didn't hire a lawyer. One was appointed to him, right? Do you remember why?" She knew the answer but wanted to verify what she *thought* she knew.

"They couldn't afford one. Something about her medical bills before the fire."

Kelli motioned to the phone.

"And now, less than two years later, she's living in a retirement home for the wealthy?"

Mark quieted as he looked through the pictures.

"Darwin and she lived in an apartment together before the fire. I remember him being asked about his residence while on stand." She held back a shudder. She didn't like recalling so many details about the trial. Yet here she was trying to remember all of the pieces. "If she was in debt with medical bills and Darwin was truly her only living relative…"

"Then how did she get the money for Appleton Retreat?" Mark finished.

She snapped her fingers. "Maybe that's why you saw a different man spreading the fire, and why Darwin didn't argue with what was going on."

Mark raised his brow before he voiced it.

"Because Darwin McGregor was paid to take the fall," he said.

Kelli nodded so adamantly that her hair swished back and forth along her cheeks.

"How much do you want to bet that her medical bills disappeared, too? How can we even find that out?" Kelli's thoughts were going faster than her reason. She certainly didn't want to give the woman a call and ask. First, that would sound alarm bells for whoever was behind this newly formed yet becoming-more-real theory. Second, Mark and Kelli definitely were the last people who should be the ones to talk to her. Even if her grandson hadn't actually committed the crime, he was definitely paying for it. Just thinking about talking to the woman started a soft loop of her sobs from the courtroom playing in the background of her memory.

Mark rubbed at his facial stubble again, falling into deep thought. He was picking his words carefully when he finally spoke.

"I may have a friend who can help us answer those questions. Though…I don't know how legal it will be."

Caught off guard, Kelli chuckled.

"Let me guess, another bodyguard friend?" she asked, already picturing the imaginary man sitting behind one of the desks she had seen in Orion earlier.

"Close, but no cigar." He handed her back her phone and pulled his out.

"So, no Orion agent?"

"No. His wife."

"Acuity Investigations. Darling Quinn here."

Mark cleared his throat as a voice he hadn't heard in half a year floated through the earpiece.

"Hey, Darling, it's Mark. Mark Tranton."

There was a noticeable pause on the other end.

"I'm not going to pretend I'm *not* surprised right now," she replied. Her tone was light and, if he wasn't mistaken, he could hear a smile in her voice. Mark relaxed his shoulders a fraction. Oliver Quinn's wife had always been a vocal woman—even before they'd married the year before—never shying away from her opinion. If she had wanted to scold him for his lack of communication with Oliver, Darling wouldn't have held off to be polite. Instead, the light tone turned concerned quickly. "Is everything all right? Is something wrong with Nikki?"

"No, no! Everything—and everyone—is fine," he assured her. "I just have a favor to ask. I know I probably don't deserve one, but if you could at least hear me out, that would mean a lot."

There was less hesitation in her reply this time. Instead of concern or cheer, Mark could hear the woman slip into work mode. Darling Quinn was a private investigator and a damn good one.

"Shoot."

"We're looking into an old case," he started. Kelli's eyes were wide with anticipation. "We think someone might have been paid off to take the fall for a fire. But…well, we don't have proof. Just the theory."

"So where is the fall guy now?"

"Prison."

Mark could almost hear Darling's gears turning. He remembered the first time he had met the private investigator. He had flown to her town in Maine to celebrate Orion's impending expansion as well as Oliver's promotion to head of the new freelancer branch. Darling had been kind, hilarious and unstoppable. It was apparent that Oliver had found his other half—the perfect partner in crime. A thread of longing started to unravel in Mark as he remembered the thought. His eyes traveled to Kelli's. Swirling pools of green and gray stared evenly at him.

Could Kelli be a perfect partner for him?

Where had that thought come from?

"Mark?" Darling asked, bringing his attention back. He looked away from Kelli.

"Yeah, sorry. What did you say?"

"I said, why do you think he was paid off, then?"

"His grandmother—his only family and the woman who raised him—went from close to poverty to living in one of those retirement homes that price gouge. You know, the ones that have the resort amenities. All after the guy's trial happened and he was found guilty."

"Curious," Darling whispered. "So you need to see the grandmother's and grandson's financials to know if he got paid and then gave it to her, or if she maybe got directly paid."

"And, if you can, the person fronting the bill."

"I guess I shouldn't remind you that tracking financials on a case I'm not currently on and without permission isn't the most *ethical* thing to do."

Mark nodded, though she couldn't see. "I wouldn't ask if it wasn't extremely important."

Darling let out a long exhalation that he didn't

miss. There was movement, and soon he heard the sound of fingers clicking against a computer keyboard. "You're lucky that Oliver is working something with Deputy Derrick right now. He'd tell me to ask more questions before I agree."

"Do you want to ask more questions?"

Darling snorted. "Too many questions sometimes degrade the degree of anonymity I like working under. Just give me the names of the grandson and grandmother, and the date of the trial."

Mark did as he was told. He gave Kelli a thumbs-up in the process.

"Thank you for this, Darling," he said after she repeated the information for accuracy. "It means a lot."

"Don't thank me—though you can later when I get back with the information. Thank Oliver. Although you've left him hanging, he hasn't stopped telling stories of the glory days."

Mark wanted to say something—something that would take away the guilt her words brought—but he couldn't find an explanation for the fact that he'd pushed his closest friends away. Instead, he thanked her again.

"I can't guarantee I'll have the info tonight, but I should be able to score it by tomorrow," she said, already typing again. "Like you, I have to call a favor in."

"No problem."

"And Mark, you know I can't keep this from Oliver," she added, voice serious. "But...there's no need to call him while we're both working. I'll just wait until he comes by after work."

"Thank you, Darling."

It was her turn to say, "No problem."

"So?" Kelli asked after they ended the call. "She'll look into the financials?"

"That's what she said."

"Wow. Just like that?" Mark scanned Kelli's face when he thought he heard a touch of jealousy in her voice. She merely tilted her head in question.

"I think Darling just likes a good mystery." Mark shrugged, hoping his expression didn't betray what he was feeling.

"Like the case against that millionaire in Maine?"

Mark laughed. "Exactly."

"I can't just wait for her to call back," she said with notable irritation. "I can't just sit still. I need to do *something*!"

Mark's thoughts led directly to the bedroom. It was so sudden and out of nowhere that he felt his expression change without the consent of his brain. How was it that the woman in front of him—wearing a zoo T-shirt and ready to pass out hell to anyone who threatened her family—could evoke such strong feelings apropos of nothing? How could he even entertain the idea of feelings for her, of any kind, when it was *his* fault that she was a widow?

Whether or not Kelli noticed the change in his demeanor, she didn't say. Instead, she slapped her hands together after a moment. A grin broke out over her lips.

"I have an idea!"

Chapter Eleven

"Can I go on record and say I really, really don't like this idea?"

Mark passed his binoculars back to Kelli, who was seated in the driver's side of her car. She was practically bouncing in anticipation.

"Believe me, you've already told me," she said with a quick smile. "Just remember—you could have said no to coming along."

Mark snorted. "Something tells me you would have still come."

He was right. She probably still would have come. But would she have gone inside? Without any backup? Probably not. If something happened to Kelli, then Grace would grow up without a mother or a father. That idea alone kept Kelli on edge as she took in the three-story building in front of them.

The Bowman Foundation's office was housed in a modern-style building on the edge of the Design District. One of the many relatively new buildings that had sprung up in the past ten years or so, the slick white office stood like a beacon of hope that welcomed those who passed by on their way to visit a market or bar, yet still added to the urban feel the District had cultivated perfectly. It was one of the many reasons the Bowman Foundation had blossomed as much as it had since Victor's spotlight had been published.

The Bowman Foundation wasn't just a charity aimed at eliminating poverty in Dallas. It was a welcoming destination to all who wanted to create a difference in the world.

"It makes you feel good when you look at it,"

Kelli commented, her eyes roaming the steel sans serif letters that composed the charity's name. "Doesn't it?"

Mark didn't bother lying. "It makes me want to help people," he admitted.

Kelli nodded, frowning. Could such an inspiring organization really be connected to Victor's death?

Mark placed his hand on hers. The contact caused her to jump, but not so badly that he addressed it.

"But I don't need to look at a building to want to help you," Mark said, squeezing her hand. The pressure started a fire that traveled up her arm and right into her face. With her cheeks fully heated, she gave him a small smile.

"We're going to find out what's going on," he said, "and we're going to keep you and Grace safe. This—this building—is just drywall and paint. You are much more inspiring."

Mark's voice was so firm, so sure, that it infused her with a feeling of confidence.

And something else.

He withdrew his hand and the moment, whatever it had been, was gone.

"Now let's go, as you said earlier, 'snoop.'" He shook his head. "I can't believe I said that."

The interior of Bowman was all clean lines, shiny surfaces and pops of color. It was more trendy than its exterior. Kelli almost forgot for a second that they were inside the office building of a charity.

A woman with a low scoop-neck black blouse and cheetah-print pencil skirt smiled at them from behind a desk that stood next to the open stairwell and single elevator. She broke her conversation with a man in a suit to greet them as they walked up.

"Welcome to the Bowman Foundation. My name is Karen." She surprised Kelli by offering her hand to the two of them. They each shook. "How may I help you today?"

The man in the suit was polite enough to pull out his phone and seem busy. Kelli cleared her throat, jumping into the plan they had agreed upon on the ride over.

"Hi, my name is Kelli Crane and this—"

Karen's eyes widened in recognition. That also surprised Kelli.

"As in, wife of Victor Crane?" she asked. The suit looked up from his phone.

A twinge of sadness hit her as she answered, "Yes, once upon a time."

Karen sobered. "I'm so sorry for your loss."

Kelli shared a look with Mark.

"Thanks," she responded. "Forgive me, but I'm a little surprised you recognized me." Unless Karen was in on whatever was happening, Kelli thought a second too late.

Karen dropped her head a fraction. "To be

honest, it was the name. I pass by that picture every day."

Kelli was confused. "The picture?" she asked.

Karen was clearly taken aback. "You haven't seen the press hallway?"

Kelli shook her head. "This is the first time I've been here," she answered honestly. She'd been invited to take a tour after their building opened to the public, but memorizing Victor's last article had been a lot different than visiting Bowman. Reading the words was easier than seeing the physical place they related to. But now that was the plan. "That's actually why we're here." Kelli motioned back to Mark. "This is my friend Mark Tranton. We both realized we had never taken a tour and were wondering if we could now?"

"Of course! Give me a quick second, if you don't mind!"

Karen hurried to the man in the suit, handing him a file before using her phone to call someone Kelli assumed was in the building. Not wanting to appear as though she was snooping—the whole reason she'd come—she fell back a step to Mark's side. The ex-bodyguard had gone tense. Kelli didn't know if that was because he was nervous or preparing himself. For what, she also didn't know, but she was grateful he was on her side.

"The press hallway?" he said through the side of his mouth.

"Yeah, I'm definitely curious now."

They waited as Karen spoke softly into the phone and the man in the suit retreated into the elevator. His interest in Kelli's name seemed to have only been a momentary thing. He didn't look up from his file as the door slid closed in front of him.

"Okay, if you're ready," Karen almost sang as she stood back up. "I'd like to start the tour by showing you the press hallway."

"All right." Kelli followed beside Karen while

Mark was a few steps behind her. She recognized his reflex to keep her safe. She wondered if that was a reaction specifically for her or if he would do it with anyone who might be in danger.

"The main floor of the Bowman Foundation is perhaps the most popular with the general public," Karen began, apparently *not* waiting until they got to the press hallway to start. "Bowman's CEO—Radford Bowman—believes that not only being out in the public but also interacting with them on a daily basis can make all the difference in keeping a community aware of its problems without bombarding them with guilt or scare tactics or propaganda to do the right thing."

The hallway they had been walking down opened into a large room. With floor-to-ceiling, wide, frameless windows on the opposite exterior walls, the space made what was clearly designated as a lounge area feel bright and airy.

As though all your troubles wouldn't stand up against such cheery surroundings. Even the occasional art piece with a quote about compassion, helping people or volunteering didn't distract from what the place was trying to accomplish.

Subtle awareness. Ample comfort.

"Wow," Kelli said as they stopped to take it in.

"The Bowman Foundation allows for this space to be open to the public for a place to relax, hang out or chat with foundation employees about what they can do to help. As you can see, we have a game area that's being utilized right now." In a sectioned-off corner of the room were a Ping-Pong table, two chess tables and a foosball table. Two young guys sat at one of the chess tables, heads bent in concentration. "We host free events with the options of donating or volunteering here, as well. The community never ceases to surprise us. We've gotten more in terms of donations from our free events than those you have to pay to get into. I know it's a little strange to give free rein to nonemployees, but by the same token, it's helped build a mutual trust and respect with those who come and take advantage of what we're offering."

"What *is* it you're offering?" Mark asked, not a curious inflection in the sentence, just a flat question. He didn't seem to approve of the grandeur, or maybe of Karen. Kelli thought she spoke of Bowman and their method of getting their community aware as a cult leader might. Sure, their end goal seemed admirable, but she couldn't shake the feeling that something felt off about it all.

Karen didn't bat a perfect eyelash at the underlying current of criticism in Mark's voice. Instead, her smile grew.

"The information to change the world without leaving your comfort zone." She turned back to the room and sighed, starting to walk again. "Isn't it wonderful?"

Mark was suddenly next to Kelli's ear.

"It sure is something," he whispered. His breath brushed against her neck and ear with such electricity that she had trouble making her feet follow Karen.

Whoa, Kelli thought, body heating. A simple whisper had stirred something she hadn't realized could stir. At least not yet. Shaking her head to try and rid herself of the unexpected feeling, she moved forward and tried to focus.

They walked the rest of the way through the lounge and then into another hallway that turned right. Kelli thought back to Victor's article as Karen slowed. The Bowman Foundation walked a fine line between the give-everything-we-own-to-help-people and let's-make-money-to-give-money mentalities. He had written that this struggle was a rare one for an organization headed by a wealthy man like Radford Bowman to have. A man like that—working his hands to the bone to rise from poverty and mediocrity, proving to everyone around him that he wasn't defined that easily—was a champion to those less fortunate. An everyday man who had become much more and could go live on an island drinking mai tais for the rest of his life but had chosen to try to make his city— his home—a better place for everyone to live. That was what made Radford Bowman a good man, and that's what made the Bowman Foundation a good organization.

Just recalling Victor's words gave her goose bumps. He had been a talented writer. He had also been a good man.

Now he was dead, and somehow the two were connected.

"The press hallway was originally supposed to be a room open to the public," Karen said as they took another turn. It brought them to a hallway that must have run parallel with the front lobby. More wide, wall-length paneless windows lined the wall to their left, while the wall to their right was covered in plaques, framed articles and pictures. "But Mr. Bowman thought it would be a better this way. He said that seeing what the foundation could accomplish shouldn't be a destination. It should be part of the journey—seeing what we can do, whom we can help—while on the way to meeting the team who could do it." She motioned to the door at the very end of the hallway. "Mr. Bowman's office."

"He doesn't use one of the other two floors?" Mark asked, clearly surprised.

Karen shook her head. Pride was evident in her reaction. "He wants everyone to be able to reach him. Sure, he could have a much bigger, better office suite upstairs, but that's just not his style." She practically beamed as she continued down the hallway to that door, pointing out a few of the articles on the wall. But Kelli had eyes only for one picture.

"Mr. Bowman thought it appropriate to dedicate a different space for this," Karen said, voice tender. They had stopped in front of a stretch of wall that squeezed Kelli's heart before she even could take it all in.

In Memory of Victor Crane was written above Victor's entire article, printed directly on the wall. Beneath that were inscribed the years he had been born and died, like his tombstone. Below that was a note that he had been survived by his wife and daughter, names excluded.

However, it was the picture that hung above it all in a beautiful golden frame that caught and held her attention so raptly. Without thinking, without being given permission, Kelli moved closer and touched the glass.

Victor Crane, frozen in time, smiled back.

And suddenly Kelli was crying.

"I'M REALLY, REALLY sorry again," Karen said. "I thought it would—I don't know—make her happy to see that we honored him, you know?"

But it hadn't. Kelli had broken down, only barely excusing herself to a nearby bathroom with tears streaming down her face. It was outside that bathroom that Mark and Karen now stood. Karen, despite her cult-like love for Bowman, seemed genuinely upset in turn that she'd upset Kelli.

"Can you give us a second?" he asked, nodding to the closed door.

"Oh, yeah, sure. I need to check the front anyway." She pointed to a door in the middle of the hallway. "That leads back out to the lobby when you're ready."

"Thanks."

Karen cast one more worried look at the door before walking away. She pulled out her cell phone, already placing a call as she went through the door she had pointed out. Mark waited a few seconds before knocking on the bathroom door.

"Kelli, it's just me," he said, voice low. Mark marveled at how, after only a few days, he thought using "just me" would work. Seeing Victor's picture…seeing Kelli's reaction…reminded him that if he had saved Victor, too, he could have spared her the heartache. Ready to stand back and give Kelli her space, Mark was surprised when the door opened a crack.

"Come in," she said, voice low like his.

He did as he was told.

The single-occupancy bathroom was small but clean. Kelli backed up to the wall next to the sink and ran a hand over her eyes.

"I'm sorry," she said, voice still a little uneven. Mark shut the bathroom door behind him and moved uncertainly in front of her. He hadn't noticed until then that she'd been wearing mascara. Some of it had run beneath her eyes. "I just—I couldn't take it. Seeing that picture..." She put her hands over her eyes and bowed her head.

Mark, compelled by an emotion he couldn't quite define, closed the space between them. He put his arms around her. Never a man to put too much stock in his intimate actions, he hoped the contact—the embrace—would bring her a dose of comfort.

"It's okay," he whispered atop her head. He felt her body tense a moment. Maybe he *had* overstepped the boundaries of their new relationship.

Kelli wrapped her arms around the small of his back and buried her face in his chest. Soft cries filled the air, but Mark didn't interfere beyond holding her. If there was one thing he knew for a fact, it was that he couldn't protect her from the ache of missing her husband.

A pain that he was finding hurt him more than usual.

A few minutes went by before Kelli collected

herself. Slowly she detached from him. Her mascara was really running now, but Mark found her impossibly beautiful.

"Are you okay?"

"Seeing Victor's picture…it opened an old wound, I admit. But I'm not sad. I'm angry," she explained, ice in her words. "I don't know a lot of things, but I do know one thing—my gut is right this time. This place—these people— they had something to do with Victor's death. And now? Now they have the gall to celebrate him with some kind of press gimmick?" Her expression turned fierce. Mark could clearly read her anger. "We have to figure out what's going on. And we have to do it now."

It wasn't until that moment that Mark realized the gravity of what they were trying to do. Or the lengths to which he would go to ensure that the Crane family got the justice they deserved.

And that Kelli and Grace would never be hurt again.

"You have my word, Kelli, that I will do everything in my power to help you. No matter what."

He meant every word.

Chapter Twelve

There was a man standing in the lobby when Kelli and Mark walked back in. She'd avoided looking at Victor's picture again. Her fear that her emotions would get the better of her again was too great. Especially considering the main emotion was unbridled anger. Mark led her out to Karen standing with the mystery man. He kept his back straight and fists slightly balled. Apparently the ex-bodyguard was now feeling that anger, too.

Kelli quickly touched one of Mark's hands before they stopped. It was her way of telling him to keep cool even though she'd just spent the past five minutes crying in the bathroom.

"I'm so sorry, Kelli," Karen said in a rush. "I didn't for one moment stop to think that seeing—well, that it might be hard."

Kelli held up her hand.

"It's not your fault," she said. "I'm sorry. I didn't realize it would be hard, either."

Karen seemed to take solace in that and gave her a little smile before turning to the man next to her.

Wearing a pressed gray button-up with a skinny black tie, a pair of pristine slacks and expensive-looking dress shoes, the man exuded importance. Older than Kelli, perhaps in his early forties, he had close-cropped black hair, brown eyes behind a pair of black-rimmed glasses and a dark complexion. His smile showed a mouth full of bright white teeth.

Maybe it was a requirement for working at Bowman.

"Kelli, Mark, this is Hector Mendez," Karen said. "He's the Bowman Foundation's publicist and PR genius."

Hector's smile widened as he shook their hands.

"I think you're taking privileges with that last title," he said, voice as cool as his attitude. "It's nice to meet you both and—" he exchanged a look with Kelli "—I'm sorry for our part in causing you any discomfort."

It was an oddly phrased apology, but she accepted it graciously. "Thank you."

"Now, Karen tells me you haven't been able to take the full tour?"

"No, I didn't make it past the hallway," Kelli joked, trying to lighten the anger she felt building inside her again. Whether it was lingering emotions or something altogether new, she couldn't tell. But she knew she wanted to leave.

"Maybe we can reschedule, if you wouldn't

mind," Mark intercepted. His hand bumped hers, and she was surprised her hand was fisted.

Play it cool, Kel.

Hector didn't seem to notice the small movement.

"How about this?" The publicist walked over to Karen's desk and pulled an envelope from a drawer. He handed it to Kelli. "I know it's short notice, but the Bowman Foundation has a dinner each year to thank and celebrate those who have contributed to us. It's formal but lots of fun. It's tomorrow—again, sorry, short notice—but why don't you two come? We can certainly do another tour if you're feeling up to it then?" Before they could answer, he added, "Our fearless CEO will, of course, be there, as well as Dennis Crawford."

That caught Kelli off guard. She scrambled to close her mouth. Had Dennis asked the Bowman Foundation about the article even though he'd told her there was no story there?

"Dennis Crawford?"

Hector looked temporarily confused. "Oh, I'm sorry. I was under the impression you two were friends? He speaks highly of you."

Kelli was quick to hide her surprise this time. She smiled. "He was closer to Victor than me, but I'll look forward to seeing him tomorrow."

Mark cut his eyes to her before adding, "Thank you for the invitation. We can't wait."

"Great," Hector exclaimed, clapping his hands together. "It should be fun!"

They said their goodbyes, and Mark and Kelli went back to the car. They didn't speak until the Bowman Foundation's building was in the rearview.

"Well, that was a roller coaster of emotions," Kelli said, breaking the silence. Her mind was being pulled in several directions, trying to figure out which thought to focus on first. She chose the mention of Dennis. "When I talked to Mr. Crawford the other day, he assured me that nothing was wrong but then wanted to see Victor's journal. I get mugged and then the house gets broken into a day later by people who probably are after the same journal. And now the publicist for the Bowman Foundation pointedly mentions Dennis will be at the dinner?"

She ran a hand through her hair. A flowery scent wafted off, reminding her of the impulse decision to use Lynn's "sexy-scented" shampoo that morning. Her motivation behind *that* action made her face grow momentarily hot.

"As a former bodyguard, I've got to tell you going to the dinner tomorrow might be a bad idea," Mark said. "Especially if the one person we suspect has a part in all of this will definitely be there."

"But that's why we need to go!" Kelli stopped

herself and amended her statement. "Thank you for standing by me in there, but you don't have to keep trying to protect me."

Kelli felt a shift in the mood as the ex-bodyguard's hands tightened around the wheel. As an afterthought, she realized with a tiny shock that he was driving her car without being asked. He'd seen she was upset and did it without mention. Just another detail that made her already scattered thoughts harder to pin down.

"You know, even when I was a bodyguard, I never *had* to protect anyone," Mark started. "I've never been forced to keep someone safe, and I'm not being forced now, either. So, yes, I know I don't *have* to try to keep you safe, but I really want to."

If his eyes hadn't been on the road, Kelli wasn't sure what she would have done with herself. Victor's picture floated behind her vision. It made her finally put the two men side by side.

Sure, looks-wise they were opposites. Victor was a lanky, almost red-haired man with a smile that approached goofy. Mark was wider—broad shoulders, solid muscles—with a no-nonsense cut to his brown hair and a little bit of a farmer's tan peeking out of his shirt. As for his smiles, they were all laced with something Kelli couldn't quite put her finger on but was finding she liked.

Personality-wise, were they also opposites?

Kelli did know one thing for sure. Victor and Mark shared one very important trait.

They had good hearts.

"I would say thank-you, but I seem to say that a lot," she answered after an awkward moment of silence had grown too loud. "So I'll skip right to the part where I ask, what's our plan?"

"Plan?"

"You know, the plan to catch the bad guy and restore justice to the world." She spread her hands out wide, making a pretend rainbow over the car's dash.

Mark laughed.

"You make it sound so easy," he commented.

She shrugged.

"If Grace can figure out how to play Candy Crush on my phone, then we can totally do this."

MARK DROVE THEM back to his apartment, where Kelli said they'd hatch their game plan. The trip to the Bowman Foundation had been much more eventful than he'd originally thought. Like Kelli, his gut had yelled at him.

There wasn't just one thing off—there were several.

"Do you mind if I go call Lynn and Grace?" Kelli asked when he'd settled into the couch, ready to brainstorm. "I'm not too good with separation from the little one." Kelli smiled a smile that clearly showed a mother's love.

"Yeah, no problem. You can go into my bedroom if you'd like."

Instantly he realized he'd made the offer sound suggestive. A Freudian slip if he'd ever had one. Kelli did a half-snort laugh and retreated into the room. It could have been his imagination, but it looked as though her cheeks had reddened. Then again, he could have been mistaken. Mark stretched out his legs and realized just how tired he felt.

Resting his head back on the cushions, he crossed his arms over his chest and closed his eyes. When Kelli was finished, he'd offer her some coffee and make a very strong mug for himself. His thoughts went from coffee to the woman who had suddenly become a part of his life.

Would she still be there after they'd somehow found the justice they both wanted and so desperately needed?

"Boo."

Mark turned his head toward the noise and slowly blinked.

Some small person was staring at him, only inches from his face.

"Boo," she said again, trying to whisper but failing.

Completely off his game and confused, he repeated the word. It made the little girl giggle.

"Grace!" The toddler whipped her head around to look toward the kitchen. She smiled even though Kelli's tone was scolding. "I told you *not* to mess with him!"

Mark, finally starting to connect the dots, sat up and rubbed his face.

"I fell asleep?" he asked, turning to face Kelli, also. His eyes widened at two things he hadn't expected to see—aside from the sudden appearance of the half pint who had gone back to staring at him. Kelli was standing over the oven cooking something—and it smelled delicious—while Nikki Waters sat across from her on a bar stool, beer in hand. "How long was I out?" he asked, alarmed.

Kelli laughed. "Um, a few hours at least," she answered with an apologetic smile. "I was going to leave to give you some privacy, but then Nikki showed up and we got to talking and lost track of the time." She motioned to Grace. "And then I started to miss that little one. Did I mention I have separation issues with her?"

As if on cue, Grace giggled. "Boo," she squealed.

"You were sleeping so solidly that I figured you'd be hungry when you finally woke up," Kelli added. "So I raided your pantry."

"And I stole a beer," Nikki said with a wink. Unlike the earlier, angrier version, this Nikki was all smiles. Her shoulders were even relaxed.

"Again, now that I say it all out loud, it sounds

really creepy…" Kelli suddenly looked panicked, just as she had when she'd first stopped by his apartment. It made him smile.

"You can be creepy all you want if it means I can eat whatever that is you're cooking," he joked. His stomach growled loudly in testament.

Kelli relaxed. "Good," she said. "I wouldn't want to be kicked out before Nikki finishes this story."

"Story?" he asked when the two women shared a look.

Nikki laughed in response. "Don't worry about it."

So he didn't. Mark sidestepped Grace and the toy that had grabbed her attention and walked to the bathroom to try to lift the postnap haze of sleep. He splashed his face with cold water and took a deep breath. A fit of laughter met his ears from the other room. Aside from the past two days, Mark hadn't had anyone come to his apartment. Especially not to eat.

Was he upset that Kelli had decided to cook dinner for his former boss, her daughter and him?

He dried his face and gave himself a good look in the mirror.

No.

He wasn't upset at all.

"Do I even want to know?" he asked after he was finished. Nikki turned toward him with another smile. Her eyes took in his freshly shaved face, but she didn't comment on it.

"Let's just say that Kelli now knows why I've learned my lesson on sending you, Oliver and Jonathan on assignments together."

Immediately Mark pictured one long drunken night in Vegas. He cringed.

"Let it be known that we had already finished a contract when we decided to try our hand at gambling," he said to Kelli, walking to the refrigerator. He grabbed a beer and went back to the couch. Grace's attention had switched to a multitude of colorful building blocks she pulled from a bag.

Taking a sip from his beer, he watched the little girl try to piece two of the blocks together. Their parts didn't connect, and her frustration was evident. He set his beer down and slid to the floor next to her. With wide eyes she watched as he took the two blocks and found a long piece that connected them. He handed the new construction back to her and she smiled.

Slowly, as if asking for permission, he took a few more blocks from the bag and started to put them together. At first she seemed unsure of the intrusion. Then she started to hand him her blocks. She scooted closer to him, and together they faced the construction of what Mark hoped would be a little house.

"A builder, a bodyguard and a gambler? That's quite the résumé, Mr. Tranton." Kelli appeared beside them with a bowl of pasta.

She held it out, uncertain. "Sorry, I know that last thing I cooked for you was pasta, but there wasn't anything else in the pantry. Also, I don't know the rules in this apartment about where we can and can't eat," she apologized.

Mark took the bowl and glanced at Grace, Kelli and Nikki. Each looked at him expectantly for much different reasons.

He smiled.

It was a definite change of pace for the bachelor.

Minutes later, all three adults were eating in a circle around a tiny block house. Grace had a bag of cereal and razor-sharp focus on a cartoon on the TV. Mark hadn't even realized he received the channel.

"Grace and I have gotten into the bad habit of watching TV after we eat," Kelli explained, sheepish. Even with the sound turned down, Grace didn't break eye contact at the mention of her name. "It quiets the toddler beast within her."

Nikki laughed. "My niece and nephew were the same way, so don't worry. Sometimes you just have to take your breaks when you can get them," she said.

"The joys of single parenthood," Kelli responded with an ounce of humor. It didn't last long, and the three seemed to remember why they were all there. Mark cleared his throat.

"Not that I'm against a visit from you, but what was it that you came to say?" he asked his old boss. As soon as the question left his mouth, he saw the woman transform into Boss Nikki. Straight back, relaxation evaporating. She set down her bowl.

"First of all, I stand by my decision to not let you look into Dennis Crawford. Especially since you're no longer an Orion agent," she said firmly. "However, after hearing your theory about the fire and realizing that someone might really have tried to target Victor and by proxy my agent, I got maternal." She held up a hand to stop his comment. "Believe me, it was a weird feeling. But it was a good thing, considering it pushed me to look into Dennis personally."

Mark's and Kelli's attention zeroed in on the woman.

"As you both know, when Orion takes on a client, we do extensive background checks on the people connected to our client. We try to find threats before they happen—something we've learned to do better since the debacle in Maine with Oliver's contract a few years ago. Since Dennis was the editor on the story and had email contact with Victor, we made sure to include him on the list of people to check out. But...no matter how hard we look or how many hypothetical scenarios we run to prepare our agents, humans have this funny way of not always adhering to the norm. They become unpredictable."

Mark put down his bowl. Kelli leaned in a bit closer. Nikki's expression sharpened.

"Dennis, I've realized now, is one of those people."

Chapter Thirteen

Silence.

It enveloped the space around the three adults. Not even the *oink* of a cartoon pig in the background could penetrate their collective concentration.

Eventually Mark spoke.

"Dennis Crawford became unpredictable? How?" He tried to recall anything out of the ordinary about the retired editor back during the contract. The only contact he'd had with Victor was through an email the day before the fire happened. It had been solely work-related and hadn't raised any red flags.

"*How* isn't as important as *when*," Nikki answered. She looked at Kelli when she continued. "After the fire, I kept our contract open and tabs on you until it was ruled Darwin McGregor was behind it. I also kept an eye on those who were closest to the case. Nothing suspicious happened with any of the people I was watching."

"The people?" Kelli asked.

Nikki paused and for a moment looked apologetic.

"Your friend Lynn, Victor's friends at the various publications he had worked with, even the last of his family—the two cousins in Denmark, Dennis and the Bowman Foundation themselves."

That surprised Mark.

"You looked into the Bowman Foundation?"

"Yes, but a cursory look that suggested they were what they said they were. Nothing more, nothing less. Dennis also appeared to act normal, considering everything." She didn't have to pause for dramatic effect. Mark was already reeled in. "Until right after the trial, when he made a few uncharacteristic choices." She held up three fingers. "First, he hired a realtor in Florida."

"He was going to move?" Kelli's eyes widened.

"As far as I can tell, he never went out there," Nikki cut in. She held up two fingers. "Instead, two, he retired from the *Scale*—in my opinion—a few years too early. And then, three, right before he went quiet, he gave a sizable contribution to a national charity organization, namely *not* the Bowman Foundation."

Mark rubbed a hand across his clean-shaven jaw. He couldn't believe what he was hearing.

"Sounds like we've got another Darwin McGregor thing going on," he observed. Nikki gave him a questioning look.

"Darwin McGregor thing?"

"We think he was paid to accept the fall for someone so his grandmother would be taken care of," Kelli said.

"And it sounds like someone else might have been paid off," he observed. "Right after the trial, almost moving, retiring early and giving money to charity?"

"Or maybe it's a sign of something else?" Nikki offered.

"Surely that can't be a coincidence?" he said, mind already set on his theory. "Having two people making choices that dramatically change their lives, all surrounding the fire? They both seem guilty of being connected."

Nikki raised her index finger. "Connected, yes, but who's to say Dennis *was* behind it all?"

Mark tilted his head toward Kelli to see what she was thinking. A storm of thought was brewing just behind her eyes. He could have looked into them for hours and never lost interest. So beautiful.

He blinked and tore his gaze away. Now wasn't the time to realize he was much more attracted to the woman he was trying to help than he would have liked to admit. He needed to focus. He needed to keep her safe.

"Listen, I'm not suggesting Dennis Crawford isn't guilty," Nikki added before Kelli could voice any thoughts. "But I am trying to put myself into his shoes. Dennis is the kind of man who loves to work—loves his job so much it's become every facet of his life. He isn't married, has no kids and probably is low on friends. Why? He's always had his nose to the grindstone. He didn't earn his position at the *Scale*. He fought to get there. Then, all of a sudden, he's not only quitting but also trying to move away? That—to me—sounds like a man running from something."

"So, what are you getting at?" Mark asked, knowing her calculations had a bottom line.

"That maybe Dennis Crawford is a victim, not a perpetrator."

Another silence took over their group.

"While you mull that over, I need to check in on a contract." Nikki took her bowl to the sink and stepped out into the hallway, phone already to her ear. She shut the door behind her, leaving the two of them together with their thoughts.

"She's right," Kelli admitted after a moment. "Dennis could be just another victim of whatever is going on. But what the hell *is* going on?" Kelli's eyes cut to Grace, hoping the girl hadn't heard her word choice. Grace didn't even realize they were still in the room. "Whether or not Dennis is a victim doesn't change the fact that he knows something."

"Then we need to figure out what that something is." Mark stood and held out his hand to her. He lifted her to her feet. Suddenly they were close. A breath or two away from each other, hand in hand. Every part of Mark seemed to awaken at the contact. It made the job of his past bringing him back to reality—pointing out that he didn't deserve to be with Kelli, of all people—harder than it ever had been before. Mark dropped their hands and took a small step back. "So why don't we just ask Dennis tomorrow?"

Kelli's eyes widened, but she nodded. "Sounds like a plan to me!"

Talk about Dennis, the fire and anything else relating to the two died down. Kelli and Mark did the dishes, and Nikki came back inside and supervised while finishing her beer. Grace became bored with whatever cartoon was on and started to fuss. She rubbed her eyes with two tiny fists.

"That's my cue to leave," Kelli said after calming the girl down. "Someone didn't get a nap, thanks to Aunt Lynn's love of torturing me."

"She's not the only one tired," Nikki said

with a yawn. "Not everyone was able to take a generous nap today." She cut a look to Mark, and the three of them laughed.

"Hey, does it count if it was an accident?" he asked.

Nikki shook her head. "You sleeping doesn't make me any less tired." She turned to Kelli, who was packing up Grace's bag. "Speaking of sleep, Thomas is refreshed and ready to go. If you're still okay with it, he can switch out with Jonathan for the night."

Kelli nodded and smiled at Mark's confusion.

"When you were out, we talked about how it might be a good idea to give Jonathan and you a bit of a break. Orion Agent Thomas comes highly recommended and has said he's more than happy to help. So, before you offer to come watch the house, let me stop you and suggest you get more than a nap tonight. Tomorrow's a big day. We need to be well rested. Or as close to it as we can be."

Mark wanted to argue—*he* should be watching over her, not everyone else—but realized that want was partly selfish. He knew Thomas was a capable agent and trusted the man just as Nikki did.

"And to entice you further to get some rest, I'll follow you home, just in case," Nikki told Kelli. "It's on my way."

Kelli smiled. "Works for me!"

And just like that, the three of them went back to their own little worlds, leaving Mark alone in his apartment.

"You sure had a full house," Craig, the neighbor, said as Mark watched the three ladies get into the elevator at the end of the hall. He had a bag of trash hung over his shoulder, on the way to the disposal. It was probably the first time since Craig had moved in that he'd seen that many people leave.

"Just helping some friends," Mark hedged, though he didn't know why he was skipping around the truth. Nikki was definitely considered a friend—an estranged one of late, but once a great friend. Kelli? They had picked back up on an acquaintanceship and found a mutual trust as they worked toward a goal. Did that count as friendship or just two lost people looking for light at the end of the same tunnel?

As Mark went back into his apartment and looked around at its emptiness, he knew one thing for certain.

He was no longer happy with his isolation.

KELLI HELD THE two coffees in her hands as if they were anchors keeping her grounded. Not physically, of course. Her legs were moving at a good pace as she walked down a hallway that was becoming rapidly familiar. But emotionally, she imagined the coffees came with strings that attached to the feelings that she might or might not have been having for the ex-bodyguard, and the invisible anchors made to keep them out of sight and mind.

Because having feelings—any kind of feelings—for the man helping you bring justice to your murdered husband was just plain complicated.

So when she knocked on Mark's apartment door the next morning, she was trying to focus on the warmth of each cup of joe against her skin instead of the fluttering feeling of excitement that she got knowing she was about to see the man.

"Good morning," she almost sang when the door opened after the second knock. It was a little too enthusiastic a greeting. She felt her face heat slightly. Mark, bless him, didn't even look surprised. Unlike the first time she'd come over unannounced, he was fully clothed. Another fun realization for Kelli: she was a little disappointed at that fact.

"I was wondering when you'd come around,"

Mark said in return, humor clear in his voice. He smiled and made a grand sweeping gesture into the apartment. "Though how you got in again, I'm not so sure."

"Your building is very friendly," she admitted. "How'd you know I'd come around again?"

He laughed and tapped his temple.

"I've picked up on your routine," he said. "The last few days, you've ended up here, so it was only a matter of time. Though I have to say I hadn't foreseen the coffee." His eyes seem to brighten as he took in the cups. "It would be a massive understatement to say that you were lucky to find anything in my pantry last night. I haven't been shopping in a week or two. That means no coffee, and I could really use it right now."

Kelli handed him a cup and was pleased at the smile that continued to spread across his face because of it. "You mean you didn't get

enough sleep last night? Even with your unexpected yet well-deserved nap?"

"I couldn't sleep that well after everyone
left." He shrugged. "I guess it was too quiet."

Instead of walking straight to the couch,
Kelli took up residence at one of the kitchen
bar stools. She tried not to feel the pull on her
heartstrings at Mark's subtle admission that
he might have missed them after they'd gone
the night before. It made her believe her theory
that maybe he was lonely after all.

She wanted to catch the culprit behind Victor's death not just for her family's justice but
also, in some way, for Mark. The more time
she spent with him, the clearer it became that
he, too, had suffered.

"So, I'm guessing Jonathan is back with
Grace and Lynn?"

Kelli nodded. "He came to relieve Thomas,
who agreed to followed me over here on his
way home," she answered. She had waved

goodbye to the Orion agent through the lobby window before he'd even started to drive away. "You Orion guys sure are polite."

"I definitely can vouch for Jonathan and Thomas. Nikki trusts them, and so do I."

"And I trust you," Kelli admitted. It earned her an appreciative look.

Which darkened immediately.

It evoked another feeling she was trying to ignore—deep concern for the man in front of her. She took a sip of coffee and readjusted her focus.

"Okay, so, tonight's goal is to corner Dennis Crawford and get some answers," she started.

"When you say it like that, it sounds so simple."

"It may be a simpler goal to meet than the other one."

"The other one?" His eyebrow rose in perfect unison with his question. The small gesture pointed out, once again, how handsome the man was. She cleared her throat.

"To get fancy, of course."

His face blanked, and it actually made her laugh.

"You'd prefer cornering a man to dressing up, wouldn't you?" She already knew the answer. "And that's why I'm here. Do you have anything fancy you'd be comfortable wearing tonight? I looked up pictures from last year's dinner." She pulled up a photo on her phone and handed it over. "Just like their building, they sure don't hesitate in being upscale."

Mark's face pinched at the group picture of men wearing tuxes and women in dresses that probably each cost more than Kelli's car.

"I have a tux," he ground out, clearly unhappy. "But I haven't worn it in a while. I don't know if it fits."

Kelli clapped her hands. "Then let's see!"

Mark eyed her skeptically. "You came over

here hoping for a movie-makeover montage, didn't you?"

"I came over here because Lynn said she could have Pretty Princess Day with Grace at her house while I saw to some errands. And you don't question when the babysitter volunteers. Though, yes, I did come over with this in mind," she admitted with a grin. "I guess Pretty Princess Day includes you, now, too."

Mark rolled his eyes skyward before shuffling back to his room, defeated. She'd already pegged him as a man who didn't take pleasure in any high-society conventions. Not that she did, either. Her thoughts slid to Victor and then his late mother. Claire had loved being a socialite. She'd attended many formal parties and events with Victor's father and then Victor with a smile on her face and happiness in her heart. Victor had told Kelli it was the confidence that she felt only when being dressed up with a purpose that had made Claire love it all.

It was a feeling Claire had tried to pass to her daughter-in-law. Before Kelli and Victor were even engaged, she'd bought Kelli a gorgeous gown so she could feel as beautiful as Claire did. She'd gotten sick and passed away before she'd ever seen Kelli wear it. Now the dress was boxed up and waiting for Kelli at the house, begging to be worn.

She only hoped she could do it the justice she should have done it years ago.

Waiting with her cup of coffee, Kelli let her thoughts do their own thing. Minutes went by before the bedroom door opened again. Kelli nearly dropped her cup. Turning without mentally preparing for what she saw next wasn't the best plan.

The mental anchors that held the strings attached to her off-limits growing feelings for the ex-bodyguard dissolved.

The tux did indeed fit.

And boy, did it fit well.

Chapter Fourteen

"That bad, huh?" Mark asked when Kelli couldn't seem to make her words work. She slipped off her stool with no amount of grace and resisted the urge to clear her throat.

Calm down, Kel! He's just a good-looking man in a good-looking suit!

"Bad? No," she exclaimed with a lot more enthusiasm than she was trying to convey. Her face burned, and she just hoped the dreary day outside helped hide the color that was surely painting her cheeks. "It's no Pretty Princess Day dress, but it definitely works."

The tux was a classic black one, tailored

to his body type. It perfectly highlighted his broad shoulders while presenting his muscles in a way that wasn't showy or vulgar. It made the man beneath the clothes go from handsome to downright sexy.

Kelli hadn't thought she'd ever find a man who made her feel this way again.

Yet here he was, fumbling with his tie, unaware of just how wonderful he looked.

"Here, let me," she said, walking over and taking hold of the open tie.

"Try and tell me you aren't surprised at the fact that I don't have a clip-on," he joked as she took both sides of the tie in her hands.

"I plead the Fifth."

Being so close to him wasn't helping her current frame of mind. She could smell his aftershave—something sharp yet pleasing—without even trying. Her hands bumped against the solidness of his chest.

"So, do you have an outfit picked out for

this shindig already?" he asked, eyes straight forward.

"Yes, but it's at the house. I also haven't tried it on since before Grace, so there's no telling how it will actually look."

"I'm sure you'll look great."

Kelli smiled at the compliment.

"We'll see. I still need to swing by there to check the job the window guy did on the office. I'm sure the new owners wouldn't like it if I left the house in bad condition." She paused, and a surge of excitement flooded through her. "Hey! Would you like to see my house?"

Mark raised his brow.

"I have?" he said uncertainly.

She laughed. "No, I mean, *my* house. The new one! Granted, it definitely isn't as big or nice, but I like to think it's cute and cozy." An odd look crossed the man's face as she finished. One that wasn't wholly bad but gave her pause. Had she overstepped a boundary? She pinned her gaze on finishing his tie. "You don't have to," she added quickly. "It has nothing to do with Dennis or the fire or anything like that. I just—" She managed a quick look up into his eyes. Their even stare pulled the truth right out from between her lips. "I wanted to share my happiness." She gave him an apologetic smile. "Sounds cheesy now that I say it."

The corner of Mark's lips lifted up. He took her hands, paused in midair and gave them a small squeeze.

"I think we both could do with more happiness in our lives." His voice dipped low as he said it, almost into a whisper. Kelli's mind jumped around as she wondered about the meaning behind his words coupled with the warmth of his skin against hers. Maybe it was her imagination wanting something she probably shouldn't have, but Mark seemed to be moving closer. Changing an already established connection to mean more.

Kelli tilted her head, angling her lips to what she wanted to be so much more than a simple kiss.

But reality decided it wasn't meant to be.

Mark dropped her hands and stepped back. Just like he'd done the night before.

She hoped she hid her hurt.

"Let me get back into some real clothes, and we can head out," he said, voice back to normal. The smile, however, was gone.

Maybe Kelli *was* just reading into his words.

HER NEW HOME was in Lake Dallas, a charming suburb that was a lot more affordable than some of the others she'd seen, and cute as cute could be. In relation to Lynn's town house, it was about a twenty-minute drive with no traffic—another reason Kelli had loved the location—but it was a good deal farther from Mark's apartment.

The latter point, she realized with a bit of

chagrin, was a blemish on an otherwise per-fect home, in her eyes.

Wrapped in gray siding, the two-bedroom home featured light hardwood floors and an open floor plan that would keep Grace in her sight from anywhere in the living room or kitchen. It was small, as she'd said to Mark, but for their little family, it fit just right.

"I like it," Mark said after she'd given him the tour. "It's charming."

"Ha. That's the polite way to say it *is* small."

"It's also the polite way to say it's charming," he countered. They were moving from what would be Grace's bedroom to the kitchen.

"Now, I know it needs a few upgrades and certainly some paint." Both their eyes cut to the olive green living room walls. "But right now we can live happily with this."

"When do you start to move in?"

Kelli sighed at that. "Technically, I could do

it now, but I booked movers for next week. Apparently I picked a popular time to move."

"You know, I'm sure I could round up enough men to help get the job done," he said, trying to be sly. "My ex-job happens to be with a bunch of bodyguards, and my current job is with a bunch of construction workers. Free labor, if you don't mind all the sweaty men."

Kelli was about to respond with a clever quip—at least, she'd try to make it clever—when Mark's attention dropped to his pocket. His cell phone was doing its vibrating dance. He held up his finger.

"Excuse me a second." He pulled out the phone and went into the backyard. Apparently he needed privacy, which was fine by Kelli. But it did make her curious as to whom he was on the phone with. Mark had admitted he was single, but that didn't mean he didn't have admirers. Aside from Nikki and Jonathan, she really didn't know if he had a social life.

She surely didn't.

While Mark was on the phone, Kelli did another sweep of the house, trying to picture where everything would go the next week. She wasn't halfway through mentally piecing together the master bedroom when a knock sounded on the front door.

Perplexed and slightly nervous at meeting who was probably a neighbor, she hurried back through the living room and opened the door.

Her stomach dropped.

"Dennis?" She asked, "What are you doing here?"

Dennis, dressed casually with a pair of sunglasses on, didn't smile. Every muscle in Kelli's body tensed. Apart from her Realtor, Lynn and now Mark, no one knew where her new house was. So why in the world was Dennis here now? Had he followed them there?

"I need to tell you something, and you need to listen," he ground out. Anger was evident in his last four words. It made Kelli step back, trying to soak up the comfort of her new home to offset her growing fear. "You need to stop digging into the past. Drop this story—it isn't one you need to tell."

"Why?" she asked, voice giving a little. "What's going on? What did Victor really find?" Determination pulsed through her at each question. She was gearing up to ask him everything right then and there.

"Victor's dead, Kelli," he interrupted with a harsh whisper. It pulled all of the air clear out of her lungs. "He found *nothing* and he still died. And now you want to know what got your husband killed? Why? So the same thing can happen to you *and* your daughter?"

"Don't you *dare* talk about *my* daughter," she said, fury filling the space left behind in her lungs. She stepped forward, aware that she was two seconds from attacking the man.

"Do you know how easy it was to find this

place, Kelli? How long do you think your body-guards will protect you and your loved ones?" That deflated her a fraction. "Can they even really protect you every minute of every day anyway? Look what happened to Victor. Who's to say it won't happen again?"

"Is that a threat?" she whispered, her confidence draining quickly.

"It's food for thought for the young mother." He bent his head down to meet her gaze. His voice was dangerously low when he spoke. "Don't go to the dinner tonight. Don't dig anymore. And give me that damn journal."

Kelli believed in a lot of things. She believed in determination and the power of self-confidence. She also believed that emotions had the absolute power to derail the other two. So Kelli, thinking of Grace and of Victor and Lynn, grabbed her purse from beside the door and pulled the journal from it.

"Don't you ever come here again," she said, pushing the journal at him.

Dennis took it but didn't smile.

"Hopefully I won't have to."

Kelli didn't wait for him to get back to his car by the curb before she was running through the house and through the back door. Mark turned at the noise and barely took her in before his entire demeanor changed.

"Let me call you back," he said into his phone, closing it immediately after. "What's wrong?"

"Dennis just came by," she blurted out, pointing wildly. "I—I gave him Victor's journal." Kelli put a hand over her mouth, instantly regretting that decision. Mark grabbed her shoulders, moving her focus back to him.

"Are you okay? Did he hurt you?"

She shook her head and then he was gone, running through the house.

Who's to say it won't happen again?

Kelli hurried inside and grabbed her phone. She dialed Lynn's number and waited for what felt like a lifetime for her to pick up.

"Is Grace with you? Can you see her?" Kelli practically yelled.

"Of course she is and yes," Lynn answered. Just like Mark, she could read the shift in the woman's mood. "Where else would she be? What's wrong?"

Kelli pulled the phone away and placed it against her chest. She took a deep breath before continuing.

"Lynn, I need to tell you something, but first I want you to promise me you'll stay inside until I get back. Please?"

Lynn, bless her, had known Kelli long enough to trust her vagueness. And to pick up on her fresh fear.

"Okay, I promise."

Mark came back as she ended her call.

"I should have fought him instead of giving

him the journal," she said without any segue. Mark grabbed her hand, a look of ferocity on his face.

"No, I shouldn't have been in the backyard on the phone. I should have been protecting you." He looked around them as if he was ready to throw whatever he could get his hands on. Luckily, there wasn't a thing to grab.

"It's not your fault he's a horrible man," she assured him. "It's not your fault I couldn't let this go. Oh, God, what have I done?" Now she was panicking. "What if Grace or Lynn or *you* get hurt because of the decision *I* made?"

Mark put his free hand behind her neck, tilting her head up. Before her panic could mount into tears, he pressed his lips against hers with such force she nearly lost her balance. The kiss wasn't entirely a kiss, she'd realize later. Like the coffee from before, it served two purposes.

One was to address the elephant in, apparently, both of their rooms. An attraction that had grown through the past few days. A bond that had been established by shared tragedy.

The second purpose was, in the simplest of terms, to focus her. To throw a cup of water in her face. To bring her back to reality.

To remind Kelli she wasn't alone and didn't have to protect everyone by herself.

A lesson she didn't think Mark had learned yet.

Mark ended the short kiss with fire in his eyes.

"It's not *you* who's in the wrong. I promise you we'll nail the guy who is."

"How?"

"I'm getting my job back."

Chapter Fifteen

"I want it to be noted *somewhere* that I think this is a bad idea." Lynn sat at the end of Mark's couch with her arms crossed over her chest, giving the eye to everyone around her. As she still wore her Pretty Princess Day pink dress and matching plastic beaded necklaces, her disapproval was almost humorous. "Heck, it isn't even really an idea, when you get down to it."

Mark had to agree with her there. His eyes traveled to his bedroom, where Kelli was putting Grace down for her nap.

"My friend at the station said that if we can prove Dennis is a threat, then we'll be getting somewhere," Nikki chimed in from her spot on a bar stool. Jonathan sat beside, her eating leftover pasta. He nodded.

"Dennis seems to be one of those guys who needs to talk," he said, careful not to speak with the food in his mouth. "It seems like all you will need to do is just walk up to him and talk. That recorder will do the rest." Everyone looked down at the little black circle on the coffee table, courtesy of one of Nikki's Orion contacts. Another benefit of Mark being employed as an agent again—Orion and its founder had quite the stash of resources. "When he incriminates himself, then just fall back to me and we'll go straight to the cops."

Lynn huffed. "So we're going to ignore the many unknowns here?" She turned her gaze to Mark. "What happens if—I don't know—he has a gun or a knife or something and decides to stop you two once and for all?" The lines in her face sharpened, her brows slamming together. It was clear she didn't even like to voice a hypothetical in which harm came to her best friend. He didn't like to picture it, either.

"I won't let that happen," Mark assured her.

"And I can't imagine Dennis would do that," Jonathan said.

"Why?" Lynn wanted to know.

"He hasn't done it yet, and he's had the opportunity. Why would he do it now *and* in front of an audience?"

Lynn slumped back into the couch cushions. "I still can't wrap my head around all of this. We still don't know *what* it was that Victor even found. What if it's all been one giant misunderstanding? A series of coincidences, and we're too paranoid to realize it?"

"I thought the same thing," Nikki said, casting an apologetic smile toward Mark. "At first I thought it was grief clouding judgment, misplaced guilt. You know, seeing signs that weren't there." She turned to Lynn. "But then we found out that Darwin McGregor received enough money to get his grandmother out of debt and into a wealthy retirement home while still giving him money in his savings a day after the trial." She held up her finger. "*That* plus Dennis's strange behavior at the same time? Whatever is going on, that man is pulling some major strings to keep it quiet. Who's to say he'll stop just because Kelli says she will?"

The room quieted at that.

Mark recalled the fear on Kelli's face as she'd told him about Dennis's visit. He had ended his call with Darling only to call back after he officially accepted his job. He'd talked to her husband.

"I'm going to skip over the fact that you called my wife and asked for help and didn't bother to at least clue me in to what's going on," Oliver had said, not giving Mark room to make excuses or apologize. "Instead, I'm going to give you a warning. I know Darling confirmed your suspicions about Darwin. He got paid. But what she didn't get was a chance to tell you she has no idea who did that. There wasn't a trace of the purse holder at all—she looked all night and morning. We even looped in Derrick with his law-enforcement connections and still couldn't come up with a name or place. Whoever is behind this—whether or not it's Dennis—they're good. They're dangerous. Watch yourself and be careful."

Now he was sitting in his apartment with the best bodyguard he knew, his boss, a very concerned best friend, a toddler and a woman he'd kissed in a heated moment. All of them creating a plan to end whatever was going on.

If he thought about it too much, Mark started to see the cracks that their plan could fall between. Lynn was right, but that didn't mean they could all just sit there and pretend everything could go back to normal. Not after Dennis had shown up at Kelli's house. Not after he had talked about Grace.

"I think this is what they make beer for," Lynn finally said. Despite their moods, it earned a laugh from the room. The weight of the unknown dangers started to lift.

"You know, I'm just curious to see what Mark's going to wear," Jonathan said. "I think the last and *only* time I saw you spiffed up was Oliver's wedding. And even then I think you changed between the ceremony and the reception."

Nikki laughed. "He did! One minute he was wearing his tux and the next he was wearing flannel," she added.

"Flannel?" Lynn asked with a grimace. "I'm a fan of flannel, but I don't think it's meant as wedding attire."

Mark held up his hands. "Hey! I didn't wear flannel to the wedding. Just the reception and, to be fair, the reception was small and at their house."

"Everyone was wearing their fanciest clothes and here comes Mark looking like a lumberjack," Jonathan jumped in, smiling at the memory.

"Please tell me you got a picture of this," Lynn said. She grinned. "I really can't picture the glory of Lumberjack Mark."

"Oh, we made him take a picture with Darling just so we'd never forget," said Nikki. She turned to Mark and her expression darkened. "Do you still have it or..."

Or did you get rid of that when you decided you didn't need friends? Mark finished her unsaid thought in his head. The past few days had shown him how easily he could fall back into step with those once closest to him. When they hadn't believed him after Victor's death it had hurt, but now he really understood their viewpoint. They had been trying to protect him from himself—from his guilt and grief—by trying to get him to move on. To stop chasing a ghost and get back to living his life. Instead of seeing it from their eyes he'd decided to believe they didn't trust him—didn't believe in him. Now, looking around at their faces, eager to help, Mark wished he could change the way he'd just shut down around them. When this was all over, he needed to do right by them.

"Of course I still have that. I still have pictures from the wedding of all of us. Including one of Jonathan trying to break-dance," he answered with a grin. Jonathan groaned in response. "Let me grab them really quick." He wanted to prove to Nikki and to Jonathan that he hadn't completely written them out of his life during the past year or so. Plus, he wanted to check on Kelli. Not being able to see her for this long didn't sit right with him. Dennis Crawford's earlier appearance had set him on edge more than he liked to admit.

The bedroom door was cracked open. Slowly he pushed inside, not wanting to knock and wake Grace if she had finally fallen asleep. The room was dark but the light from the window—even though it was cloudy—lit it enough that he was able to make eye contact with Kelli when he walked in. She and Grace were both lying down. Grace's arms were wrapped around Kelli, and her eyes were closed.

Mark pointed to his closet and tried to get there as quietly as possible. Within the walk-in he found the shoebox he'd labeled as Doliver—his name mash-up for the Quinns—and started to slip back out of the room.

"How's it going in there?" Kelli whispered. Her voice cut through the silence like a knife. He turned, surprised she had said anything at all. "Don't worry. Once she's like this, we could sit here and recite every episode of *Dora the Explorer* and she wouldn't wake up. This one sleeps hard." She smiled. "Want to keep

me company until the octopus decides to de-
tangle from me?"

Mark stifled a laugh and nodded.

"If that's a pickup line, I can honestly say
I've never heard it before." He kicked off his
shoes and put the box down on the floor before carefully lying down on the opposite side
of Grace. Both adults watched her with wide
eyes. She stirred but didn't wake up and didn't
detach from her mother.

"Bullet dodged," Kelli said once Grace had
stilled again. "She may seem like a pretty chill
child, but if you wake her up before she's had
enough rest, she'll show you just what war
looks like. And we have enough on our plates
right now. Speaking of war, how are our troops
out there?"

Mark settled his head back on the pillow and
looked at the ceiling.

"We've gone over the plan enough—not that
it's complicated—and everyone's ready. Lynn

thinks we shouldn't go, and I don't think so, either," he admitted.

"You think it won't work?"

"No, it probably will. Jonathan thinks Dennis will say something to us when he sees we came despite his warning. I agree."

"So, why shouldn't we go, then?"

Mark turned his head to face her. Her green-gray eyes still managed to be clear in the low light of the room.

"Because Lynn's right, too. What if he pulls something and *does* try to hurt you?" Mark felt the backup of words behind his tongue. Words that needed saying, emotions that needed out. But was it the time? Was it the place? Would it ever be?

"Then you'll stop him. You'll protect me," Kelli answered simply. The uninhibited trust she placed in him was so pure that Mark couldn't stop what he said next.

"I couldn't protect Victor." Kelli blinked. She

hadn't expected him to say that. He could see the surprise clearly on her face. He took advantage of the lag and continued. "If I had, you wouldn't need protecting now. Not by me. I'm so sorry, Kelli."

The anguish—the guilt since the fire—had finally burned its way through his skin. Lying there with Victor's wife and daughter was too much for the bodyguard. He needed Kelli to know that *he* knew he had let her down in an unimaginable way. He could no longer deny that he had feelings for the beautiful blonde. Like his admission now, the kiss earlier had sprung from an inner desire he could no longer suppress.

Expecting her to finally see reason—her trust might really be misplaced—Mark started to get up. It shifted the bed enough to jostle Grace. Before he could clear her reach, the toddler flipped from her mom and grabbed his arm. He froze, and like the little octopus she was, she looped her arms around his and buried her face against his shirt.

Mark remained steady until it was clear she had gone back to sleep. He wanted to do at least one good thing by Kelli, even something as small as not waking up the toddler. However, he wasn't used to affection from a child. Even if that child was fast asleep. He looked at Kelli uncertainly.

She smiled, and the room around her seemed to brighten.

"Mark, I'm only going to tell you this once, so please take it to heart." She put her hand in his, resting them both against the sheets. "I *never* blamed you for Victor's death and I *never* will. In my eyes, you did your job perfectly." She squeezed his hand before moving hers over Grace's hands on his arm. "Do you want to know why I think—no, why I *know*—that?"

Mark nodded, transfixed by her words.

"Because, no matter what else you did that night, at the end of it you saved me. Which means you saved Grace." Without heeding her own advice not to move her child, Kelli leaned across the girl and brushed her lips against Mark's. The kiss was so soft he almost thought he'd imagined it as she pulled away. "And for that, I am eternally grateful. So, as Victor's widow, I have to ask you to stop blaming yourself for every wrong thing that has happened and might happen. If Victor could talk to you now, he'd tell you the same thing. I *promise*. It's time for you—and me—to stop living in that tragic past." She paused and looked down at her daughter. "It's time we start focusing on a more beautiful future." She reached up and took his chin in her hand. "No more of this tortured-soul stuff. Okay?"

A chuckle rose in his throat as if her touch alone had absolved him of a burden he'd carried for two years. Ever since the first night he'd held her in his arms and carried her to safety.

"Okay," he agreed. A smile that felt better than any he'd had in a while pulled the corner of his lips up.

Kelli mimicked it.

"Good." She backed away from him slowly, rolling over and carefully getting out of bed. "Now you stay with the octopus while I take a look at you as a lumberjack." She went straight for the box he'd put down.

"Were we that loud?"

She mocked surprise. "Oh, I didn't tell you? Along with mom separation anxiety I also have mom hearing. It's a bundle thing." She opened the box and pulled out the photo album. "We know you can pull off a tux, but now let's see if Mark Tranton can pull off flannel."

Chapter Sixteen

Afternoon quickly turned into night, and the humor the small group had been enjoying quickly disappeared. It was getting time to put their plan in motion, even if not all of them thought it was a good plan to start.

"This concern comes from a place of love," Lynn said from the edge of the bed. She had made a clothes run and had now changed out of her Pretty Princess attire and into a pair of jeans and a white-and-yellow blouse that contrasted beautifully with her dark complexion. Her half of the best-friend necklace Kelli had bought them when they were in high school hung around her neck in plain view. Occasionally they would don them when they were nervous about something involving one another. The last time Kelli had worn hers was when Lynn had a job interview. The last time Lynn had worn hers was when Kelli had gone into the hospital to be induced for labor. In a way it was like a good-luck charm.

"If you weren't concerned, *I'd* be concerned," Kelli said. "But we need to stop Dennis. I don't trust him, Lynn."

The other woman sighed and nodded. "Yeah, yeah, I just…" She pursed her lips, seemingly choosing her words carefully. "Remember when you asked me to be Grace's godmother?"

Kelli laughed. "Of course. You baked a cake for us to celebrate."

"Exactly! I was so excited—so honored—to get the title that I didn't really think about what it meant until today. After you told me what was going on." Kelli tilted her head in question. "If something happens to you, God forbid, I'll raise that kiddo so well, you would be proud. That's a promise I made, but it's not one I *want* to fulfill." Her eyes started to mist as she continued. "You and Grace are my little family, and if something happens to you—"

Kelli closed the space between them, enveloping her friend in a warm embrace. Lynn wasn't a woman to cry easily. She didn't look down on the emotional, but she wasn't typically gushing about her own feelings. To see her almost cry—to hear her sniffling back tears—almost brought Kelli to her own.

"He might come after Grace, Lynn," Kelli said. "I won't sit around and wait to see. I have to do this, but I need you in my corner. I need your good vibes."

"Then let me come with you two," she said, pulling back to look Kelli in the eye. "I have that obnoxious orange dress back at home that

I could wear!" But then Lynn stopped herself. "Grace," was all she said.

"I trust Jonathan and Nikki, but Grace trusts you. I need you here and so does she."

Lynn hung her head a fraction and sighed again. "I guess I should start up with those good vibes, then."

Kelli clapped, and just like that they were on the same page.

"That's the spirit," Kelli exclaimed. "Now, let's start with this dress, or was it a mistake to put this thing on?"

Kelli went to stand in front of the closet door. The full-length mirror showed her a reflection she wasn't used to seeing.

Her hair hung in loose curls, framing a face with impeccable dark eyeliner and red, red lips—thanks to Lynn, despite her concern— and coupled with long, skinny silver earrings. Though how could anyone focus on her face when she was wearing the dress?

Constantly getting dolled up and stretching her socialite muscles might not have been Kelli's forte, but she couldn't deny her appreciation for the dress wrapped around her. Navy blue silk slid across her body, starting out strong with a breathtaking deep-V back and ending with a small but elegant train. It also dipped into a much more modest V at her chest, showing limited yet undeniable cleavage. The sleeves were short and cupped the top of her shoulders while the rest of the dress hugged her body, forcing her to rethink her undergarments when she'd first put it on. Her shoes—which couldn't be seen beneath the rich fabric—in no way compared. They were fifteen-dollar black pumps that had more than one spot where a marker had come into play.

"Is it too much? Or am I underdressed?" Kelli asked, recalling the picture of the women from the past year's dinner.

"It's just beautiful," Lynn answered. "You're

going to make it really hard for Mark to concentrate."

Kelli turned at the humor in her voice. Lynn smirked. "Don't think I've missed this—" she waved her hand in the air at Kelli "—getting all weird when he's mentioned or in the room."

"Weird?"

"It's a good weird. I just haven't mentioned it yet because I wanted *you* to bring it up, but— since you didn't and you're about to go talk to a psycho while wearing a ball gown—I'll go ahead and tell you that I think it's time you grabbed some happiness of the intimate kind." Lynn's smirk transformed into a caring smile. "I approve of this Mark character. He's a good guy, you know. But that doesn't mean we aren't going to talk more about this when it's all over."

If it had been anyone else, Kelli might have blushed. However, it was Lynn, so she just laughed. Of course the other woman had picked up on the change between her and the bodyguard.

"Deal."

"Good! Now let's go showcase this elegant-as-all-get-out dress!"

Kelli gave herself one more look in the mirror. The dress truly made her feel beautiful, but beauty wasn't the goal for tonight. Getting a man to admit to his sins was their true endgame.

Instead of Lynn letting Kelli simply walk out into the living room where Mark and Grace were, she decided to announce it.

"Lady and gentleman, may I present to you Pretty Princess Kelli!"

Mark stood from the spot where he'd been playing blocks with Grace and not so subtly looked her up and down.

"You're beautiful," he said, face openly appreciative. Heat swarmed up and filled her cheeks.

"You're not too bad yourself." She motioned to his outfit. Like earlier that morning, he was the perfect picture of sexy in the classic tux.

"Sure beats your flannel," Lynn said.

"Har, har." Then, like flipping a switch, his mood did a complete one-eighty. "Jonathan went ahead to find a good spot to wait and watch," Mark said, brows drawn in focus. "Nikki is on her way up. All we need to do now is put this on and head that way ourselves." He scooped up the recorder and looked her up and down again. She could have sworn she saw him turn a bit red.

"I'm pretty sure that thing won't be able to fit in there or stay," Lynn commented.

"We still need it on you just in case Dennis decides he'll only talk to you when I'm not right beside you."

"She's right," Kelli agreed. "*I* barely got in this thing."

A knock at the door paused whatever Mark

was about to say. He checked the peephole—twice—before opening the door to let Nikki in. She looked between the two of them and whistled.

"Well, don't you two look nice?"

"Thanks, but we've apparently hit a snag. There's not a good place to hide this." Kelli pointed to the recorder. "I guess I could always put it in my clutch but, depending where I set it during dinner, that might look suspicious."

Nikki held up her hand. "I think I have a fix for that." She walked over to the kitchen counter and set down the bag she'd been carrying. The three of them huddled around her.

"Orion is all about using nonlethal methods to ensure client safety, because we believe our agents can handle any type of fight," she said, sounding rehearsed. "Our agents are well trained and experienced so the clients don't ever have to make contact with their aggressors. However, sometimes exceptions can be made." She pulled out what looked like an older cell phone and looked at Kelli. "It's a stun gun," she said. "On the off chance you need—or feel like you might need—some help. It looks somewhat like a phone, so it will blend."

"Somewhat?" Kelli shared a matching look of surprise with Lynn. "If you hadn't told me, I would have tried to make a call on it!"

Nikki laughed. "Don't worry. I would have stopped you."

Mark cracked a smile. "I would have, too, if it's any consolation," he said.

"And I appreciate that, but what does a stun gun have to do with hiding the recorder?"

Nikki held up another item from the bag. Black cloth and elastic made up a two-inch circle with a small slit in the middle.

"Is that a garter?" she asked.

"Of sorts." Nikki took the stun gun back and slid it into the slit so it wouldn't fall out. She took the recorder and put it into a small pocket on the back Kelli hadn't seen before. "These are popular with women who want to carry their phones or cash without having to take their purses around. We're just tweaking that idea with stun guns and recording devices." She handed the garter to Kelli. "Now to try it on."

"I FEEL LIKE A SPY."

Kelli patted her silk dress above her right thigh. The light from the city filtered through the Jeep's windows and showed a slight bump beneath her hand.

"Just make sure when we sit down to put a napkin over that, Ms. Bond," Mark said, eyes sliding back to the road. Kelli snorted.

"Is it bad I'm kind of hoping I can use the stun gun? I've never used one before."

"As long as you don't use it on me, we'll be fine."

Kelli stopped fidgeting with the garter filled

with goodies and started to rub her hands to-gether instead. She was nervous and trying to hide it. Mark wanted to tell her it would be okay, but he knew it wouldn't do any good. In her mind, they were going into enemy terri-tory, and he couldn't exactly disagree.

The rest of the car ride was spent in silence. It wasn't unpleasant, just two people caught in their own thoughts. Mark wondered what the woman was thinking about. *He* should have been thinking of the situation at hand, but his mind seemed to be sticking to her.

When he had told her she was beautiful be-fore, it had been partially a lie. What he should have said instead was that she was the *most* beautiful woman he'd ever seen. It wasn't be-cause of the dress or the way her hair curled. It was the smile of modesty and the dose of vulnerability that had made every part of his attention attach to her. Kelli Crane was a strong-willed, fascinating woman. She contin-

ued to surprise him with her loyalty and concern for others. Also able to see his internal
pain, she'd had the compassion to try to quell it.

And she had.

And then some.

Her speech and her kiss had dislodged an affection for the woman he was finding he would
like to keep beyond whatever happened tonight.
But did she feel the same? Was it just the heat
of the moment moving them down this path?
Could they be together once she didn't need
protecting anymore? The bodyguard didn't ask
any of these questions.

Now wasn't the time.

They had work to do.

The Bowman Foundation was lit up like a
Christmas tree. Even at night, it felt like the
epitome of hope, bright and promising to those
who needed it. None of this surprised Mark as
he parked the Jeep and took in the surroundings. Cars filled the parking lot. Two men in

suits stood outside the doors, clipboards in their hands and smiles on their faces.

"Hopefully we're on the list," he said, trying to get her attention away from wherever her mind was focused. It worked. She laughed a little and turned. Unease lined her expression. It was a look he didn't like at all. "Kelli, we don't—"

"Mark, this is possibly the best way to get Dennis to condemn himself," she interrupted. "So, we do have to do this. I don't want Dennis ever to show up at my house again. I won't live in ongoing fear for Grace's safety."

She patted her thigh one more time and got out of the truck. Mark took a deep breath and followed.

Aside from the men at the door, he didn't spot anyone else outside the building. Jonathan was doing a good job at hiding.

"My lady," Mark said. He held his arm out.

"It's been a long time since I walked in these

heels, so I truly thank you," Kelli said, laughing. She linked her arm through his.

Together they walked right up to the lion's den.

Chapter Seventeen

Kelli's head swam.

Pain and confusion. That's all she could wrap her mind around at first. What had happened? Where was she? Why did her head hurt so much?

Darkness invaded the space around her, clinging to her skin like a blanket. Blinking several times didn't help. She still couldn't see a thing. The darkness was thick. Unrelenting. Terrifying.

Where was Mark?

She desperately tried to remember what had happened. The life before this darkness. But she was too panicked to concentrate. The pain in her head didn't help matters, either.

Calm down, Kel, she thought sternly. That phrase was becoming her mantra, she realized. What she also realized absolutely killed any attempt at calming down.

She couldn't move.

She was tied to a chair.

"Oh, my God," she gasped. Her wrists were pulled behind her, tied together. She tried to move them but they were anchored to the back of her seat. As she twisted her hips, her stomach dropped. She was tied to the front two chair legs from her shins to her ankles.

Wherever she was, it wasn't good.

"Hello?" she asked timidly—afraid of who would answer, afraid that no one would.

"Kelli!"

If her stomach dropped before, it absolutely crashed through her and the floor at the voice beside her.

"Lynn? Oh, God, is that you, Lynn?"

"Yes! Yes, it's me."

Kelli almost cried in acute fear. She forgot to breathe for a moment.

"Grace?" she asked, every hope and prayer in her world resting on one name.

"She was still in the apartment with Nikki. She should be okay," Lynn said hurriedly. "I was the stupid one who left it."

Relief flooded the mother's heart. She wasn't completely calm, but she was in a better state of mind to work with whatever happened.

"Are you okay?" Kelli asked.

She could hear the other woman trying to move around. "He beat me up pretty good—I think my lip's busted—but I'll live." Lynn paused, then added, "I think."

"Who beat you up?"

"I don't know his name—all I was doing was taking out the trash—but he shoved me into the elevator and just attacked." Lynn's voice wavered. "I shouldn't have left the apartment, but I was trying to be nice since Mark let us stay in his place! I'm sorry, Kel. I should have stayed with Grace."

The maternal voice of reason within Kelli agreed, but the woman who loved her friend like only family could defended her.

"Nikki will realize something is wrong. She won't leave Grace to come get you. She'll call the cops," Kelli reasoned. She hoped it was true. She prayed it was true. "Do you know where we are?"

"No, the guy slammed my head into the elevator wall, then nothing but stars. Are you okay? What happened?"

Kelli tried her restraints once more. They didn't move an inch.

"My head hurts a lot," she admitted, giving up. "Everything's fuzzy. I remember walking into the Bowman Foundation with Mark. We talked to a few people—everyone was mingling before the dinner actually started—" She closed her eyes tightly, trying to remember. "We were looking for Dennis but ran into the publicist guy who said he hadn't shown up yet. Ugh, my head." A wave of nausea passed over her. She opened her eyes, but the darkness kept her disoriented.

"What else?" Lynn prodded.

"I went to the bathroom and—and it was out of order," she continued, words coming faster as her memory was catching up. "I was told to use the one up the stairs." She remembered leaving the second-floor meeting room and walking into the hall. Her heels had been loud as she hurried to the steps. The publicist had said it wasn't too long a trip. She'd see the bathroom door as soon as she reached the top and turned. "I got to the top but there was a man there! He was waiting for me!"

"Who was he? What did he do?"

Kelli shook her head, instantly regretting the action.

"He was wearing a mask—a ski mask." Then it clicked. "He was wearing all black, too, just like the man who broke into the house...just like the man Mark said he'd seen at the fire." A sick feeling began to spread throughout her. "I tried to run," she continued after an involuntary gulp. "But I didn't get far. He threw a punch that I apparently didn't dodge." Now the pain in her head made sense.

"We both were knocked out, brought together and tied to chairs," Lynn summarized. "But why? And where do you think we are?"

Kelli didn't answer. Instead, she listened for a moment.

Silence.

"I can't hear anything," she whispered, "and our mouths aren't bound like the rest of us. And I really can't move—whoever did this took their time—so for them not to gag us, too?"

"Means we're probably not where help could hear us if we screamed," Lynn answered.

"Right." Kelli felt panic flare. Her heartbeat thumped much faster than normal.

"The guy who grabbed me wasn't Dennis Crawford," Lynn whispered. "I didn't recognize him at all."

Kelli let out a long breath that shook at the end. "That means our plan was never going to work," she admitted. "All of this was pointless. We don't know what Victor found, we don't know why it's bad and we don't know who put us here. We're not even back to square one." Kelli's fear bled into the tears brimming in her eyes. "I'm so sorry for getting you mixed up in all of this, Lynn."

"No. Don't you go all soft on me," Lynn shot back. Her voice was hard, pointed. "We aren't going to sit here and play the blame game, especially since none of this falls on either of us. Okay?"

Kelli nodded but remembered the woman next to her couldn't see her. "Okay."

Another bout of silence fell between them. Kelli tried her best to keep her thoughts away from her daughter and the fact that if anything happened to Kelli and Lynn, Grace would end up an orphan. Thoughts of the bodyguard weren't any better. Worry clutched her heart as she wondered where the man was and if he was okay.

You can't lose it now, she tried to yell in her head. *Mark will save you. He'll rescue both of you from the dark. You'll see Grace soon.*

But no amount of self-assurance could stop the sheer terror that seized her body at what happened next.

Another voice sounded in the darkness, so close she could feel the breath the words rode on.

"I guess it's time to break this silence and tell

you why exactly you're here," he said. "And why you definitely won't be leaving."

Light filled the room. Kelli blinked past her fear and focused on the man across from her.

"Oh, my God."

THE WOMAN CHATTING his ear off was named Maria Something-or-Other. Mark tried to be polite as he scanned the ever-growing group in the large room, but the older woman was starting to grate against his already sensitive nerves. Kelli had taken the easy way out and escaped to the bathroom. He'd tried to follow but had found it trickier than it should have been to detach from the older woman. When Kelli came out she'd be surprised to see the two partygoers chatting right outside the door.

"It's nice to see the younger people start to give back," Maria said after another large sip of her champagne. "I only wish my son were as charitable. Do you have any kids, Mr. Tranton?"

If she hadn't said his name, Mark probably would have just kept nodding along.

"No, I don't."

"Good on you," she said with vigor. "Enjoy as much as you can before your wife and you decide it's the right time. Me? I wish I'd waited a few years. Traveled and such." Maria kept on with that thought, not giving Mark the room to interject that he wasn't married. Not that he'd tell her that, though. She—along with a few other guests whom they had talked to after first coming in—had made the assumption Kelli was his wife. And that didn't really bother him, he was finding out.

Mark scanned the large room once more, taking in the new and old faces of the fifty or so guests who had arrived already. Round tables with white tablecloths and centerpieces made up of succulents and burlap—something Kelli had pointed out was simple yet beautiful—took up the entire room, leaving only enough space against the far wall for a grand piano and its pianist to perform while everyone mingled. They had wondered why the dinner wasn't served in the chic lounge downstairs. Publicist Hector had answered that question when asking if they liked the more "intimate" setting. The room was indeed smaller than the lounge. It forced people to talk to each other instead of doing what Mark was trying to do. He just wanted to stand in the corner and not talk to a soul who wasn't Kelli while waiting for Dennis finally to show.

Maria was somewhere in a conversation that involved the topic of margaritas on the beach when Mark flipped from nonchalance to outright concern.

"Maria," he interrupted, making her pause midword, "can you do me a favor and go check on Kelli? She's been in there for a few minutes."

Whatever offense she might have taken at

being interrupted was lost when she realized she was needed. She smiled wide.

"Isn't that sweet," she almost cooed. "Of course I'll go check up on her."

The older woman swished her long dress away with her, disappearing into one of the two public bathrooms next to the meeting room opening. Mark kept his eyes glued to the partygoers. The dinner wouldn't start until the CEO made his grand entrance. Apparently he couldn't be bothered to mingle. Dennis was still nowhere to be seen.

If he didn't show, they'd have to come up with a different plan.

"Are you sure she went in there?" Maria asked a moment later. Mark looked down at her, confused.

"She said she was going to the restroom," he answered, replaying Kelli's words in his head. But he hadn't actually seen her walk in there, had he?

"Well, we would have seen her leave," Maria reasoned. "So my guess is, she never went inside."

Mark let out a breath that was filled with bad, bad words and left the wide-eyed woman behind. If Kelli wasn't in the bathroom, and he knew she wasn't in the meeting room, then he had no idea where she would be. Guilt and shame coursed through him as he pulled his cell phone from his jacket pocket. He shouldn't have let her out of his sight—bathroom be damned.

Moving out into the hall, he fully planned on calling Kelli and, if she didn't answer, bringing Jonathan in, but apparently the bodyguard *and* their boss had already called several times.

"Son of a—" he ground out, realizing he'd silenced his phone by accident. Such a small mistake might cost him big. Temporarily ignoring the missed calls from Jonathan, he called Kelli.

Her phone went straight to voice mail.

Mark fisted his hands, already starting to walk down the hallway. There were a few offices on this side, in the opposite direction of the main stairs. He called Jonathan while he quickly looked in each one.

"Jonathan, I need you to—" Mark started as soon as the phone picked up.

"Mark, Lynn was taken," Jonathan interrupted.

The bodyguard stopped in his tracks.

"What?"

"She apparently decided to take the trash out and didn't come back."

"Is Grace okay? Nikki?"

"Yeah, Nikki didn't want to chance leaving her alone, so she locked up and called me. I'm over here now."

Mark's relief made him start to move again.

"How do you know Lynn was taken?"

"There was a bag of trash from your apartment strewn next to the elevator...and in the elevator there was some blood."

"Did you call the manager to look at the security feed?" Mark knew each floor had cameras positioned at the ends of the halls. The apartment complex prided itself on safety.

"Yeah. Too bad the room where the feeds go was broken into and vandalized," Jonathan said, clearly unhappy. "I called the cops, Mark. With or without proof of what Dennis has been doing, a woman was kidnapped."

"No, you did the right thing," he assured his friend. No sign of Kelli down this side of the hallway. He turned back and hurried for the stairs. "I can't find Kelli," he admitted, grit in his voice. "She went to the bathroom and never made it inside. I lost her, Jonathan. I had one job and I lost her."

It was Jonathan's turn to suck in a breath.

"I'm on my way."

"No, you stay with—" Mark stopped mid-sentence. Past the open stairs that connected all three floors, walking out from around the corner of a hallway was none other than Dennis Crawford.

Meeting Mark's stare, he stopped.

The bodyguard felt rage boil within him.

Dennis wore a tux, much like Mark, but with one blazing difference—he had a bloody nose. Like someone had busted it trying to fight back.

Before Mark could deal with what his next step would be, Dennis turned tail and ran.

The bodyguard was right behind him.

Chapter Eighteen

For the second time in as many days, Mark had to rely on speed rather than brawn. Dennis had run back down the hallway he'd come from—a hallway that was long, narrow and straight—giving Mark enough time to reach the retired editor at the end of it.

"Where is she?" Mark roared. He grabbed the man by the scruff of his jacket and pulled back. It was an attempt to throw Dennis to the ground—to stop him—but the man was quicker than he looked. He spun around and threw a punch that landed squarely along Mark's jaw.

The pain made him let go of Dennis's jacket. He braced for another hit.

It didn't come.

Dennis pushed through the door next to them while Mark scrambled after him.

The door led to the service stairwell—concrete steps and metal railings—and Dennis seemed to know exactly where he wanted to go. Instead of taking the easier route to the first floor, he started to jump the steps two at a time to go to the third. Mark didn't have time to question the motivation behind the more difficult escape route.

He just wanted to find Kelli.

Dennis jumped three steps and was out the door to the third floor door so fast, Mark was afraid he would lose Dennis completely if Dennis knew the layout of the building. Mark ran up the stairs, feet pounding. The sound that echoed back was almost deafening.

But not so loud that he missed the gunshot that rang out ahead of him.

On reflex alone, Mark stopped and ducked down, waiting for the second shot off. Instead, what followed was an eerie quiet.

How had Dennis gotten a gun so fast? Had he been hiding it?

Something wasn't adding up.

Mark crept up to the open door and looked down the hallway, ready to duck back in at a second's notice.

What he saw *definitely* didn't add up.

Dennis was leaning against a closed door a few feet away, hand holding his side. He was facing the empty hallway ahead of them. Mark waited a moment to see what else would unfold. With his free hand, Dennis pawed at the door handle next to him. He was hurt—that was plain to see.

Confused yet cautious, Mark hurried up behind him, still ready to react if needed.

"I just realized what you said down there," Dennis said, voice low. "You asked where she was. You're the bodyguard." The man turned slightly, keeping his hand on the knob. Mark was about to restrain him when he saw the blood beneath his other hand. He'd been shot in the side. Mark's eyes whipped up and over the older man's shoulder toward the end of the hall-way. Who had shot him? No one else seemed to be around. "Unless you have a gun, I sug-gest we hide," Dennis said, managing to get the door to open. Mark got ready for the ambush he was sure was going to come from the other side but instead was met with a dark office.

"What's going on?" Mark didn't understand anything. "Who shot you?"

"I did," a voice called.

Mark's training made him react faster than his brain could process the man in black step-ping around the corner at the end of the hall. He grabbed Dennis and pulled him inside the office as another shot rang out. Mark slammed the door shut, locking it. He threw the light switch and turned on Dennis.

"What the hell is going on?" he asked again. They were standing in a small office with a wooden desk in the middle, two lounge chairs against the wall and a potted plant in the corner. There were two doors in the wall to their right. One open to show a sink and the other closed with a plaque that read Connie Cooper, IT.

Mark immediately went to the latter and cursed when it was locked. He looked back at Dennis, waiting for a response.

"I was trying to protect Kelli and Grace," he said, face contorted in pain. "And myself."

"From what?" Mark wanted to know. If Dennis wasn't the kingpin behind everything, then who was?

The man in black—who had become Mark's nemesis in every way—yelled in the hallway.

"It's time we had a little talk, Mark. There are a few things I'd like to say!"

Mark felt his eyes widen. The night kept getting more confusing.

"What?" Dennis asked, apparently alarmed by his change in expression.

"I know that voice," Mark whispered. Recognition turned to disbelief and then to anger. The man in black was Craig. "He's my neighbor."

KELLI BLINKED AGAINST the harsh light, but the man in front of her was as clear as day.

The Bowman Foundation's own publicist genius, Hector Mendez, was grinning ear to ear.

"My, don't you look lovely," he said, voice sickeningly sweet. "And yet how troublesome you are."

"I don't understand," was all Kelli said.

Hector straightened his tie and shrugged. "And yet, you continued to try and figure it all out," he said. "You can only dig so long before you're just left with a hole that needs to be filled."

The analogy sent a shiver up Kelli's spine, but she held his gaze firmly. Hector tilted his head to the side. It made him look unbalanced, which she was figuring was an accurate assumption to make about him.

"Even now you're trying to work it all out, aren't you?" he asked. "Though who can blame you at this point? Let me start by saying a quick hello to Miss Bradley." He looked at Lynn. "My apologies for my associate, who seems to have gotten a little too happy bringing you in."

Kelli turned to look at her friend. Her lip was indeed busted, there was a cut along her eyebrow and blood had dried on her forehead, along her hairline. Kelli felt her maternal instincts flare. She wanted to protect her best friend—wanted to ensure her family's safety—but couldn't do either if she stayed as scared as she was. Seeing Lynn's wounds was a shock she needed. She rounded on Hector.

"Let her go," she demanded. "She never did any of the digging. It was all me. She knows nothing."

Lynn started to say something, but Kelli shot her a look that froze the sentiment on the tip of her tongue. Kelli didn't know what the outcome of this bleak situation would be, but she needed at least to ensure Lynn's safety. Kelli needed her to be all right. And so did Grace.

"Sadly, I'm not going to do that," Hector said with little empathy. "From what I can tell, even if I were to let Lynn here go, she'd never let *this* go." He motioned to the room around them. It was used as storage. Boxes lined the wall. "Her best friend tortured and killed in front of her? Yeah, I doubt you'll let that go. What do you think, Miss Bradley?"

The anger Kelli had felt changed to dread.

"You bastard," Lynn growled.

"I've been called worse, trust me." Hector detached from his spot against the wall and threaded his fingers together. Moving them quickly, he popped them and sighed. Their current situation had him unfazed. Like *this* was a normal day at the office for him.

And maybe it was.

"I don't understand," Kelli tried again. "How are we a threat if we don't even know what's going on?"

"Threat?" He snorted. "You aren't a threat. An annoyance, but not a threat. Your husband wasn't even a threat, really. He was just a damn fine reporter." Kelli felt her body tense. Hector didn't miss it. "Does it please you to know that you were right about Victor's death? Does it make it hurt any less?"

"So you did set the fire?" Kelli ventured, anger starting to grow.

"I didn't, but yes, it was my call. An unfortunate but necessary precaution."

Kelli shook her head. "Why? What did he find? Was it because of the names in the article?"

Hector's smile shrank. He pinched the bridge of his nose, clearly annoyed, and closed his eyes.

"He found an error in judgment. One I made and refuse ever to pay for." He massaged from the bridge to the top of his nose before opening his eyes again. "I'm afraid I'm not answering your questions to the best of my ability, am I? Well, too bad. It's time for you to answer me some questions. For starters, who all have you talked to about your theories? How many people have you shown the journal to? I need to know exactly how many loose ends I need to tend to."

Kelli set her jaw. "If I tell you, will you let us go?" she asked.

Hector laughed. "Let you go? Oh, no, we're

way past that," he sneered. "I don't like loose ends and you definitely need to be tied up."

Another series of shivers danced up Kelli's spine.

"Then why would I answer any of your questions?"

"Simple." He moved over to stand in front of her before bending down so his eyes were level with hers. "This—all of what's about to happen to you—will be a demonstration of what I will do to your daughter if you don't answer *every single question* to my satisfaction. Is that clear?"

She had no time to answer—no time to let the words or anger or absolute, all-consuming fear to sink in—before a distant *bang* made all three of them look toward the door.

"What the—" Hector was up and at the door in a flash. He pulled his cell phone from his pocket, dialed a number and put it to his ear. Whoever picked up, it was fast. "What's going on out there?" There was a man on the other end, but Kelli couldn't make out what he was saying. She chanced a glance at Lynn. Her eyes were wide with fear. "Your incompetence is outstanding," Hector practically yelled. "Take care of it. I'll send you backup, but I'm leaving." He ended the call with force. "It looks like no torture tonight," Hector said, obviously upset.

Another *bang* echoed in the distance.

"Or at least, I won't be the one to do it."

Without another word, Hector opened the door and left, closing it behind him.

"Those were gunshots, Kel," Lynn said. Her voice was low, terrified.

"I know."

They waited for another shot to sound. It didn't. After a moment, Lynn spoke again.

"Again, remember Marcie Diggle's fifteenth birthday party?" Surprised at the question, Kelli looked at her friend. Her eyebrow rose, but she nodded. "This isn't as bad. Unless they—whoever 'they' are—suggest we play spin the bottle with Gordon Taylor again, we'll be okay." Lynn gave her a smile. It was small and weak, but it was a smile nonetheless. "Despite our current situation, all I can think about is that boy's excess saliva. Yeah, this has nothing on that nightmare."

Kelli couldn't help the laugh that escaped. It was also weak. The world had become horribly complicated in the past few days. "We've sure been through a lot."

Lynn nodded. "Whatever happens to us, Grace will be fine," Lynn assured her.

Kelli felt tears start to prick behind her eyes. She jerked her head to say she agreed. An image of the little girl smiling back at her filled her head.

"I love you, Lynn," Kelli choked out, her composure cracking.

"I love you, too, Kel." Lynn's voice wavered.

It hurt Kelli's heart.

"Now, let's agree on something," Kelli said, trying to tamp out the tears.

"Okay."

Kelli cleared her throat. "We fight like hell when they come for us."

MARK KICKED THE door clear off its hinges with the idea that practice makes perfect. Connie Cooper would not be happy on Monday.

"We don't have a gun," he said to Dennis, walking away from the downed door. His leg was slightly sore, but the pain wasn't anything alarming. He was happy to know he had done it without any issues—that he was strong enough to do it on his own. "And we don't have another way out."

He moved back to the door that led to the hallway. No thundering footsteps, but Craig was still coming their way.

"Do you know if the girls are up here?" Mark whispered.

Dennis stood in the bathroom doorway, a hand towel pressed against his bullet wound. He was growing more and more pale.

"Yes, but I don't know which room."

That was all Mark needed. He unclenched his fist, still holding the phone from his call to Jonathan, and tossed it to Dennis.

"Call the cops. Then call the contact named Jonathan Carmichael. Tell him everything you know," he ordered. "Got it?"

Dennis caught the phone with his free hand and nodded. "What are you going to do?" he asked.

"I'm going to save Kelli."

There was no time to elaborate. The doorknob started to turn. Mark took up position.

"Why don't we get this over with M—" Craig started. Mark didn't let him finish. Praying the man wouldn't shoot, the bodyguard reared back. He kicked the door for all he was worth. Instead of coming off its hinges as easily as the last—his practice door—this one largely splintered. Mark pushed forward, using the top half of the door as a projectile aimed right at the gunman's head. It caught Craig off guard, giving Mark enough time to kick the bottom half of the door out of the way. He launched forward and kept the top half against Craig, forcing him down to the ground.

Mark rolled to the side once the dust settled, ready to fight the man for his life. But Craig wasn't moving. Mark scanned the wreckage for the gun. He spotted it on the other side of Craig, inches from his open palm. The body-guard didn't waste time in grabbing it.

Training his new weapon on the man at his feet, Mark kicked off the piece of the door. Craig had thrown his mask away already, con-firming exactly who he was and how much damage he'd just taken. With a busted nose matching Dennis's, he also had a busted eyebrow and cheek. Mark had hit him with a lot more force than he'd originally thought.

Craig moved his head to both sides before opening his eyes. They looked enraged.

"What? Going to shoot me, neighbor?" he seethed.

Mark put his shoe on the man's chest to keep him from jumping up. "Where are they?" Mark ground out.

The downed man chuckled. "Even if I told you, would it matter? It's not like I came alone."

Mark's eyebrow rose, silently questioning him, when footsteps sounded in the corridor Craig had come from. Mark wasn't going to catch a break.

Two men popped around the corner, and Craig yelled what clearly was an order at them.

"Kill Kelli Crane!"

Chapter Nineteen

When the men came for them, Kelli and Lynn were both on the floor, having tipped their chairs over toward each other in a fruitless attempt to escape.

Now, staring up into the faces of two strangers in suits, Kelli understood that fighting wasn't an option either woman had.

"Watch the door," said the man closest to Kelli. His partner nodded and went back outside. The first man pulled a gun from beneath his jacket and pointed it down at her. *Grace is safe*, Kelli thought, closing her eyes. Lynn started to yell at the man, tears in her throat.

Bang! Bang!

Kelli's eyelids flew open. The man outside the door dropped, his upper body falling in the middle of the doorway. The man above Kelli redirected his aim.

"Who's out there?" he called.

Like a savior descending from the sky, Mark Tranton answered.

He ducked around the door frame and shot.

The bullet hit the man's arm, forcing him to drop his gun.

"Move and I'll shoot again," Mark warned. But the man didn't listen. He let out a guttural growl and charged the bodyguard. Mark had lied. Instead of shooting him again, he stepped back when the man was close enough and clocked him a good one upside the head.

The man crumpled to the ground.

"Kelli? Lynn? Are you okay?" he asked, rushing inside. He knelt by Kelli and began to work on the rope around her wrists.

"We're a thousand times better now that you're here," Kelli almost cried, relief coursing through her veins.

"Man, do you know how to make an entrance," Lynn added, just as clearly overjoyed at his timing.

"It's Hector Mendez, Mark," Kelli said after he freed her hands. He set her right side up and then moved to Lynn while Kelli started to work on freeing her legs.

"The publicist?"

"Yes. He wouldn't tell us why he's doing this, but he definitely seems to be the mastermind."

Mark untied Lynn's hands just as Kelli freed her legs. Her head was still swimming, but she managed to help Mark right Lynn and untie her legs.

"A different man grabbed me, though," Kelli said.

Mark nodded, disgust showing in his face.

"He's my neighbor. I've already had a run-in with him."

"Does that mean we're at the apartment complex?" Kelli realized she still didn't know.

With Lynn's restraints off, the three stood.

"No, we're still at Bowman. On the third floor."

"What about Grace? Is she okay?" Kelli found all of her hope riding on the outcome of his answer. She wasn't disappointed.

"I talked to Jonathan. He said she's safe with Nikki and the cops." Kelli was enveloped by a hug from Lynn.

"Thank God she's okay," Lynn cried.

Mark reached out over her friend's shoulder and took Kelli's chin in his hand.

"I agree."

Kelli felt her lips pull up into a small smile. Mark mimicked the sentiment before dropping his hand.

"Now let's get out of here."

They stepped over the two still men, following the bodyguard closely. Kelli knew that what she'd heard earlier were gunshots and she'd even seen Mark shoot the man in the room with them, but still she wouldn't look at their bodies to confirm if they were dead or not. Knowing, she guessed, would welcome in even more panic at their situation.

"Are we going to take the stairs?" Kelli whispered. She didn't think they'd be able to get out of the building undetected if they took the stairs that split the building in half. There was no telling how many people wanted their silence. They needed to get out of Bowman and fast.

"Yes, but the service stairs," Mark said, picking up on her concern. "We need to make a quick pit stop first."

The two women didn't question him.

They hurried down the length of a small hallway, past offices and a lounge, until it turned right. Mark came to a stop before they rounded the corner. He motioned for them to stay back and pulled the gun up, ready.

He peeked out.

Kelli tensed in worry.

"Son of a—"

Lynn grabbed at Kelli's hand while Kelli fisted the other. She hadn't been ready for the man in black earlier, but now there was no question about how far these people would go. If Mark hadn't come in when he did…

She squared her shoulders.

Now she was ready.

"He's gone."

Kelli gave Mark a look split between confusion and fear. Lynn met his words with an equal amount of both. Seeing the two of them look up to him, count on his words and his protection, filled him with a determination so fierce that he doubted he'd need the gun to get them out of the building.

"Who?" Kelli whispered. There was blood dried near her scalp. She'd been hit there hard.

"Craig," he answered, looking back down the empty hallway. "Stay behind me," he reiterated. No one complained.

Slowly, yet not too slowly because he had no idea how many people were working with Hector, the three crept down the hallway to the debris pile. Mark spotted blood on the carpet, but there was no way to tell where Craig had gone from there.

"What happened to him?" Lynn asked, eyeing the splintered pieces of wood.

"I threw the door at him."

"You threw the *door* at him?"

Mark didn't have time to explain further. He held his hand out to get the women to stop. Peering around the empty door frame, he looked into the office for the man in black.

It was empty.

"Dennis?" he called, still trying to keep his voice low.

"Dennis?" Kelli asked, voice *not* low. It made Mark turn back to her.

"He's on our side."

Kelli's eyebrows went sky-high. If Lynn hadn't had one of her hands, he was sure she would have put them on her hips.

"And how the hell do we know that?"

Movement out of the corner of his eye pulled his attention back into the room. The closed bathroom door in the office opened. Dennis met his gaze and gave a weak smile.

"Because Craig shot him."

Mark moved the party into the small room and took his phone back from the wounded man. Even though the bodyguard hadn't been gone long, Dennis's condition had undoubtedly worsened. Pale and covered in sweat, he kept his hand and the towel beneath it pressed firmly to his side.

When he saw Kelli and Lynn, Mark saw relief wash over him.

"I don't understand any of this," Kelli said to the room. Her expression had softened at Dennis's obvious pain. But not by much.

"We need to leave, now," Dennis said, ignoring her and talking straight to Mark.

"What we *need* are answers," Kelli persisted. She detached from Lynn and walked around Mark. Her anger—her frustration—was running over. Shoulders straight, jaw set, eyes unblinking. Mark wanted answers. Kelli needed them.

Now.

Dennis let out a long, shuddering breath. It made him wince. He refocused on the woman in front of him.

"In short, Hector Mendez has been using the foundation as a cover for drug running. Even shorter—half of the organization is in on it, which means that half of this building probably wants to kill us." He turned to Mark. "Which, again, is why we need to leave. Right. Now."

There was a moment of stunned silence. One that Mark was guilty of partaking in. The Bowman Foundation was a cover for drug running? Who was privy to that knowledge? Who was working for Hector?

The situation, although already on the bad side of the scale, seemed much more dire.

Mark grabbed Kelli's hand.

"Did you do what I said?" he asked Dennis.

"Yes. I called the cops as well as that Jonathan guy. I told him the short truth but then had to hang up." He looked past them to the door debris. "I heard him moving." Dennis looked apologetic. "I didn't want to get shot again."

Lynn, who had fallen back to the door, let out a weird squeak.

"Guys, hear that?" she asked, eyes wide.

Mark listened.

The footsteps were heavy and loud. At least two men were running down the hallway they'd just come from. No doubt thanks to Craig.

"Someone's coming," he said. "We need to get out of this damn building!" Mark pictured waves and waves of men with guns spreading through the building like a virus, trying to find the four of them. At best he had three bullets left. Even if they decided to hide until the cops came, there wasn't any insurance that they would be safe. They were in Hector's territory, not his.

"The only way out is down the service stairs," Dennis pointed out.

Mark nodded. He didn't want to have a standoff now and waste bullets that he might need later. Plus, he didn't think he'd ever be able to recreate his Hulk smash through the door. "Let's go!"

Mark ran into the stairwell through the still

open door. Quickly scanning the concrete steps and listening, he deemed them a much better option than where they currently were. He motioned to his flock to move inside the stairwell and start descending. Kelli and Lynn were fast. Surprisingly, Dennis wasn't too bad, either.

Mark shut the door and reestablished himself as the leader.

He needed to be on point if he wanted to protect them.

To protect Kelli.

They managed to clatter all the way past the second-floor door when the third opened with a *bang*.

"Stop," a deep voice bellowed above them. The space between the stairs was wide enough that Mark could see two faces—two *new* faces—peering over the railing. He could also see a gun pointed down.

"Go, go, go," Mark yelled.

Loud cursing from above filled the air as

their small group was steps away from the door to the first floor. Mark reached out, ready to open it, when a bullet hit the concrete a step away from him. He recoiled and redirected his feet down the rest of the stairs to the last landing, out of view of their pursuers. The door was labeled Basement, Employees Only.

Mark flung the door open and ushered Kelli, Lynn and Dennis inside.

The basement—a floor he hadn't thought existed—was the complete opposite of the building that stood above. It was cold concrete with dim lighting. Mark bet that not many of the Bowman Foundation employees ventured to this uninviting place. Also unlike the rest of the building, this floor didn't seem to have long parallel hallways. Instead, everything was disjointed—more doors than seemed necessary chopped up every walkway.

Mark went to the left and started to navigate through the layout until he was comfortable there were enough doors between them and their hunters to talk.

"I don't think the elevators reach this level, so I'd have to hope there's a second set of service stairs," he said, slowing to look around another turn before making it. "We reach it, get to the lobby and get the hell out of here."

Mark glanced back at his motley crew. All three were out of breath, but Dennis was panting. Bent over slightly, he put his hand against the wall when they paused.

Kelli didn't miss Mark's summarizing look.

"He needs help, now," she whispered, grabbing Mark's hand and squeezing it. Whatever anger she'd harbored against Dennis seemed to be ebbing away.

"We have to keep moving," Mark answered loudly enough for the other two to hear. "They can't be too far behind us." He squeezed her hand back and pulled her along as he continued forward. Their shoes became a desperate rhythm as they hurried toward a stairwell that might or might not have been there.

The hallway forked and gave them the option to continue forward and turn right, doubling back, or turn left. Mark definitely didn't want to double back. Hiding on the third floor was an entirely different ballgame from hiding in a dark, empty basement. Its lack of easy access was enough to put the bodyguard even more on edge. So Mark took the second option and peered around the corner to the left.

"Found the stairs," he called back. The door marked Stairs was like a light at the end of a tunnel. "Let's go!"

Finally, he thought, *some good news.*

"Mark," Lynn shrieked.

The bodyguard spun around in time to see Dennis stumble sideways, eyes barely open. Mark moved backward to catch him under one arm while Lynn caught the other. He wasn't fully unconscious, but his knees were buckling. The towel he'd been holding fell to the floor, a bloody mess. Kelli didn't hesitate to pick it back up.

"Keep pressure on it," she told Lynn. Lynn was about to do just that when the stairwell door banged open.

Craig's chest heaved. Blood trickled down his face. Mark's good news hadn't lasted long at all.

Craig smirked.

It made something in Mark break.

"I see you still have my gun," the man said with obvious disapproval. "Are you going to shoot me in cold blood in front of these fine young ladies? Or maybe you can use one of these doors instead?"

Mark's hand twitched. The gun felt heavy in it.

Shooting Craig, no matter how badly he wanted to put the crazed man out of commission, wasn't a good move. Not only did Mark want to save what ammo he had left for the un-known trek across the lobby, but also he didn't want Kelli and Lynn to see him shoot the man. Plus, they still needed answers.

Mark hadn't missed Kelli's attempt to not look at the men he'd already hit upstairs.

No, he thought with determination, *I can take him on my own.*

"Kelli, take this and go hide," he whispered to her. Surprised but perhaps on the same wavelength, she took the gun he held out. Mark dropped out from under Dennis's arm. Kelli re-placed him, bolstering the weight of the nearly unconscious man between her and Lynn. "Use it if you have to," Mark urged her.

Kelli looked as though she was going to say something, but Mark didn't have time to lis-ten. They were in a building potentially filled with men who *needed* their silence.

Mark, however, had no intention of staying quiet now.

Chapter Twenty

If Kelli had known how active her night would be, she definitely would have purchased a more flexible dress. As it was, she shuffled along a new corridor, trying to balance Dennis's weight with the pressure to find a hiding spot, and quickly. She hadn't forgotten about the men who had originally forced them into the basement.

"Let's get into a room," Kelli said to Lynn. The shorter woman was having a more difficult time supporting the tall man. It would be much easier to hide him and then hide themselves… but Kelli was realizing she didn't want to just leave him behind. She still didn't know the full extent of his involvement with what had really happened, but Mark had seemed to trust him. Plus, her maternal instincts were in full gear.

Dennis was hurt. Badly.

He needed to be protected.

"In here." Lynn nodded to a door near the end of the hallway. Kelli held most of Dennis's weight as her friend slowly opened it and peeked inside. "It's dark."

"Good."

They struggled inside before Lynn shut the door behind them.

"Should I try the light?" Lynn whispered. Fear coated her words. Kelli couldn't deny that the darkness made her heartbeat race even faster. The last time she was in a dark room, Hector had been there.

Waiting.

"Yeah, just to see what we're dealing with."

Lynn fumbled against the wall for a moment before flipping the switch.

"Oh, my God," Kelli breathed.

It was a long room that—if she had to guess—was the heart of the basement. That wasn't the only thing it was the heart of—it was easy to see the room housed an insane amount of drugs. Bags of white were boxed across a long table that ran most of the length of the room. Scales sat on the cabinets that lined the wall opposite them, along with boxes that were closed, taped up and marked Bowman Foundation, Providing Hope, Providing Light.

"Why wouldn't they lock *this* door?" Lynn whispered, more panicked than before.

"We need to hide in a different room," Kelli responded instantly, already trying to open the door again. Dennis didn't move with her and instead went completely limp. Kelli wasn't prepared for the dead weight, and together they fell to the floor. Like the rest of the basement so far, it was just painted concrete. Pain exploded in Kelli's elbow as it connected with the floor that just wouldn't give. Dennis slumped on top of her. At least she'd been able to break his fall.

"Crap," Lynn squealed. She crouched down and tried to pull Dennis back up. "He's so heavy for such a lean guy!"

Kelli wasn't going to argue with that.

"Let's set him up against the wall," Kelli said after taking in a few breaths. Together the two heaved and pulled the man into a sitting position, propping him up as best they could against the wall next to the door. Kelli moved the man's jacket out of the way to see the extent of his wound.

"Oh, man, oh, man," Lynn chanted beside her. "That doesn't look good."

"Don't pass out, please," Kelli scolded. She took the towel Dennis had been using and pressed it against the wound, setting the gun down next to him.

"I almost passed out once when I accidentally *saw you giving birth* and I've heard about it forever," Lynn said in mock offense. She was trying to lighten the mood. "We're in a room filled with cocaine in the Basement of Doom and I'm still hearing about it."

Kelli wanted to smile—she wanted to laugh—but Dennis wasn't looking good. And Mark...

The last she'd seen was him walking toward the man who had killed her husband. She hadn't wanted to leave him, but at the same time she'd known that staying would distract him. Plus she needed to get Lynn and Dennis safe.

"Put your hand on this," Kelli ordered, her mind wholly on Mark. He'd saved her life and now was fighting to keep it safe. Lynn, despite her aversion to blood, did as she was told.

"What do we do now?" Lynn asked.

Kelli stood and surveyed the room. She really didn't like that they had chosen it to hide in. Aside from the door they had just come through, another door at the far end led back out in the direction of the first set of stairs. Another door was opposite it, nearer her. Did it connect to the hallway Mark and Craig were in?

She had to find out.

Kelli nudged the gun on the floor with her foot. "Put that in your hand and shoot anyone who tries to shoot you," she said, another order in a voice she hoped was stern.

Lynn's eyes widened. "Where are you going?"

"To help Mark. I can't just leave him to fight for us." As the words left her mouth, she felt a surge of emotion swell and surround her heart. "I can't leave him," she said more softly.

Lynn could have pointed out that there wasn't much Kelli might be able to do. That he'd made them leave. That she was a distraction. All of the things that Kelli was currently thinking… but Lynn didn't.

"Shouldn't you take this, then?" she asked instead, holding the gun back out to her.

A weird clicking noise cut off Kelli's response. The two women turned toward it.

"No," Kelli whispered in anguish. Someone was turning the doorknob at the other end of the room. The one farthest from Mark. The other men who had chased them had found them. The knob twisted, and both women fell silent in fear. However, the door was locked.

"What do we do?" Lynn whispered. "We can't just leave him here, can we?" She looked down at the defenseless man. His breathing was shallow but he *was* still breathing.

"No, we can't. Come with me," Kelli snapped. "I have a plan and it's probably really stupid."

Lynn didn't question her. She put Dennis's hand against the towel on his side and quickly followed Kelli right to the door. The knob had stopped turning, but jingling could be heard from the other side. They were going to unlock the door.

Kelli hiked up her dress and put Lynn's hand on the fabric.

"Pull," she ordered. Momentarily confused at the weird demand, Kelli caught on quickly. The two pulled their handfuls of fabric in two different directions. They didn't stop until it ripped open up to Kelli's thigh.

Where Kelli could grab Nikki's stun gun with ease.

She pushed Lynn to the side so she wouldn't be seen when the door opened.

"Use the gun if you have to," Kelli whispered.

The jingling of keys stopped as Kelli slid off her shoes and aligned herself to the left of the door. She gave Lynn one quick nod and turned off the light.

The sound of metal scraping metal filled the large room.

Kelli tightened her hand around the stun gun and waited.

Keep calm, Kel. You can do this.

The door unlocked and opened. Even though Kelli would realize later that what happened next was quick, in the moment everything slowed down. Light from the hallway came into the room, but not enough to tip the men off that two women were waiting for them. The man in front took a step inside and reached toward Kelli to flip the light switch.

That's when she acted.

Squeezing the buttons on both sides, she pushed the stun gun into the man's chest. It crackled to life. The man never saw it coming. He dropped the gun in his hand and spasmed to his knees.

"What the hell?" his partner yelled from behind.

Kelli turned, ready to zap him, too, but he was faster. He caught her wrist and twisted hard. She screamed in pain and, like the other man's gun, the stun gun fell to the ground. Kelli brought her foot up in an attempt to kick the man away from her, but he anticipated the move. He slung her down to the ground next to his partner using only her wrist.

Pain once again exploded within her elbow as it connected with the ground.

But pain was nothing compared to the fear that washed over her.

For the second time that night, a man had her on the ground, gun in hand.

"It's amazing how one woman can be such a pain in the a—" he started.

"Ahh!"

Lynn let out a war cry as she rushed the man. Even though she was short in stature, the force of her body hitting his slammed him into the opened door. Kelli scrambled to her feet and lunged at the man's gun hand. She tightened her grip around *his* wrist and tried to shake the weapon free. He thrashed around, dislodging

Lynn and nearly knocking Kelli back down. If he moved like that again, she'd lose her grip and he'd surely shoot them both.

So Kelli took a page from the Grace toddler handbook, craned her neck over and bit the top of his hand.

"Are you serious?" the man roared in pain. Kelli bit down harder just as he used his other hand to grab her hair. He yanked back, which did the trick. She yelped in pain, releasing her hold. "It's not so fun, is it?" he spit out. Kelli was sickened to hear a touch of humor in his voice.

"It sure isn't!"

Two *thuds* sounded.

Then Kelli's attacker crumpled to the floor.

Chest heaving, breathing painfully quick, Kelli stumbled over the man she'd shocked and felt for the light switch. When she finally found it, she winced at the pain in her wrist.

The men—the same ones dressed in suits

who had chased them into the stairwell to begin with—were sprawled out next to each other. The first one who had been shocked was facedown, arms bent awkwardly away from his gun. The other was slouched against the open door with blood on his temple.

"Why didn't you use your gun?" Kelli asked Lynn. She scooped up the stun gun and the first man's weapon. The stun gun went back to her garter. It was warm to the touch.

"I did," Lynn exclaimed.

"You pistol-whipped him!"

Lynn bent to retrieve the other discarded gun.

"I panicked! Excuse me for not being all Miss Bad Butt Stun Gun Lady," she said with a huff. "But hey, we started with one gun. Now we have three, so that has to be helpful, right?"

"I sure hope so."

MARK SLAMMED INTO the wall so hard that for a moment all he saw was stars. It didn't help that

Craig wasn't giving him any breathing room to defend himself—let alone hit him back. Since Kelli, Lynn and Dennis had gone to hide, the man in black hadn't let up.

Apparently he'd been partaking in a lot more gym sessions than Mark had realized.

The bodyguard ducked to the side as Craig aimed a punch his way. Instead of connecting with his face, it hit his shoulder. The pain that came from that added to a growing list of aches radiating throughout his body.

He brought up his bloody knuckle in an undercut to the man's stomach. Craig wheezed and staggered backward. He wasn't unstable for long.

Craig was fast—Mark would give him that—but he was also arrogant. Mark had been in a lot of fights throughout his life and he knew Craig's type. He fought with the confidence that no one else could win. That he was invincible. That, even though Craig's eye was bloody, his torso probably sore and his knuckles bleeding, Mark was still going to lose.

He was wrong.

Mark met him in the middle with a one-two punch to his jaw. Craig blocked before his fist could connect beneath his chin. The bodyguard countered at the same time Craig threw his punch. Mark's fist hit the other side of his jaw just as Craig dealt a jab into Mark's brow.

Mark felt the blood before he even felt the pain.

Both men broke apart, each in their own worlds of hurt. Warm liquid streamed down into Mark's left eye, stinging it. He wiped it away with the back of his hand and cringed at the pain. He could have sworn he'd heard a crack but hoped Craig had only busted his eyebrow.

"You know, I could have killed you more times than I care to count over the last two years. I should have." Craig backed up a few steps, rubbing the length of his jaw. "But no, Hector said you didn't know anything. That you were harmless." He laughed and spit to the side. Blood mingled with his teeth. "I bet he'll be singing a different tune when he finds his men upstairs."

"So—what?—Hector paid you to kill Victor and then become my neighbor? Sounds like you're whipped," Mark shot back. As much as he wanted to end the fight, he needed to catch his breath. If that meant keeping the man talking for a second and finding out some answers, then so be it.

Craig's nostrils flared.

"Call it an offer of convenience. I needed a place to stay and he needed someone watched for a while. Don't mistake that for blind obedience. I don't work for anyone," he seethed.

"But I thought Boss Hector *was* pulling all of the strings?" Mark prodded. "Or is breaking into a house to steal from a woman and child something you like to do as a hobby?"

"Like you, bodyguard, I have *clients*," he said, a smile starting to seep through his words. "Unlike you, I know how not to destroy their lives completely." His tone gave way to a wide grin. "They don't resent or pity me."

Mark recalled the soft touch of Kelli's lips earlier that day.

The all-consuming guilt he'd felt for the death of Victor was one he'd never forget. However, that didn't mean it would keep him from living. Trying to cut Mark down by reminding him he hadn't saved Victor wasn't going to work. Not anymore.

If anything, it made his resolve stronger.

"You're right," Mark said. It was his time to smirk. "You should have gotten rid of me when you had the chance."

This time Mark was the faster of the two. He grabbed the man's shirt collar with both hands and head-butted him hard. Craig let out a howl of pain and fell to the ground.

Ready to finish the fight—to knock the man out of commission—Mark went for him again. Craig didn't try to back away or move to the side. Instead, he grabbed at his ankle and produced something that went beyond leveling the playing field to downright demolishing it.

Craig held the small revolver steady as he struggled to his feet. There was no smile left in him.

He was all pissed.

"You had another gun?" Mark asked, frustration and anger clashing inside of him.

"Welcome to Texas!"

Chapter Twenty-One

The good part about fighting in such a narrow space was that the only way Craig could easily escape was by backtracking several feet before fleeing through the stairwell door. On the flip side of that coin, Mark was in the same boat. To get out of view or range of the gun in Craig's hand, Mark would have to run backward and hope he could turn around either corner before the crazed man got a shot off. The other option was to rush him but, by the look in Craig's eyes, Mark knew he'd be shot in the process.

So Mark quickly weighed his limited options as Craig got to his feet. His gun never wavered.

He raised his hand a fraction, getting a better bead on Mark's head. The bodyguard tensed.

He needed to move—to disarm the man—or else Mark wouldn't be able to protect the people in the basement counting on him.

To protect Kelli.

"I'm done with this," Craig ground out. Blood stained his teeth as he spoke. "You're not worth all of this trouble."

Mark bent, ready to charge, when a loud *bang* sounded.

He froze. He hadn't been fast enough. He was too late.

Craig had shot him and now he was going to die.

Mark waited for the pain or the darkness that introduced death to overtake him.

But it never came.

Craig dropped his gun arm to his side and fell awkwardly to his knees. Even though he was wearing black, the bodyguard could see blood blossoming right above his stomach. Craig's wide eyes traveled over his shoulder.

"Drop the gun or I'll shoot higher next time," Kelli demanded, voice even. Mark whipped his head around.

Kelli Crane was absolutely fierce.

She stood barefoot, legs braced apart, both hands holding the gun with an almost perfect stance. Her hair was wild, and he couldn't help but notice that her dress had a new slit showing almost all of her bare leg. He wasn't as thrilled about the blood he could see dripping from her elbow, but there was no doubt that Kelli was holding her own. And then some.

Mark's attention went back to Craig as he dropped his gun. That got Mark moving. He closed the space between them and picked up the weapon. The sound of Kelli's bare feet slapping the concrete echoed around them as she surprised Mark once again. She pushed past him, put her foot on Craig's chest and kicked.

He fell backward with a groan.

"That's for threatening my daughter and hurting Lynn." She reared back and kicked him in the groin. He rolled over with a yell. The bodyguard cringed. "That's for hurting Mark." She lowered the gun at him. "That bullet is for me," she whispered, voice so cold it froze Mark to his spot. Was Kelli really going to kill Craig? Would he try to stop her? Could he?

She took a deep, shuddering breath. Luckily, he wasn't going to have to find out. Without turning, she handed the gun back to Mark. "And the fact that I'm not going to kill you right here and now is for Victor. He'd give you mercy, a courtesy you didn't extend to him or his family."

Kelli turned to Mark with one unmistakable expression written across her face.

Relief.

"Are you okay?" she asked. Her tone had warmed up considerably.

"Thanks to you."

A small, tired smile tugged up the corner of her lips.

"Do you think you can carry him into that room?" Kelli motioned to the door behind them. It was offset to the right so he had to move to the side to see it. That was probably the reason Craig hadn't noticed Kelli walk up at first.

"Yeah, but I think we should get going before anyone else catches up to us," he advised. The two men who had chased them into the basement must be somewhere close.

Kelli's smile grew a fraction.

"Believe me, I think we have enough firepower between us now that we'll be okay until the cops get here." She sobered. "Dennis is fading. I don't think we need to move him any more."

Mark nodded after some consideration. The possibility that they'd be met with more force in the lobby—or even the stairwell—was high. At least they had two guns now. If they holed up in a room, then waiting wouldn't be as stressful.

"Don't worry about being gentle with him," Kelli said when Mark reached for a still-writing Craig.

"It didn't even cross my mind."

KELLI HADN'T EXAGGERATED when she said they had enough firepower. She watched Mark's surprised expression with a bit of pride as he took in Lynn standing near the two downed men with a gun in each hand. After calling Jonathan and updating him on their location, he got the entire lowdown of what had happened from Lynn.

"Maybe you should think about joining Orion," he said.

Kelli shrugged. "When you back Mama Bear into a corner…"

Mark laughed. She realized how happy the sound made her.

A few minutes passed before a sound she *wasn't* happy to hear met their ears. Footsteps were pounding across the concrete in the hallway they'd just left.

In a flash, Mark raised the handgun Kelli had used to shoot Craig, Kelli grabbed the revolver Craig had almost used to shoot Mark and Lynn pointed both her guns all at the doorway. They were done messing around.

"Whoa, whoa! I come in peace, guys!" Jonathan Carmichael held his hands up in surprise at the scene when he opened the door. "When you said you had this, I was assuming you were just trying to seem manly in front of the ladies, but damn!"

With Jonathan came a flood of police and two EMT groups. One dispatched upstairs to check on the downed men there. The second came for Dennis and the others.

"Take him first," Lynn said to one of the EMTs. She pointed to Dennis. "He's the good guy, not them."

And they did just that.

Finally, escorted by Jonathan and the head of police himself, Kelli, Mark, Lynn and Dennis made it out of the Bowman Foundation. Lynn gave her statement in the parking lot before asking to be dropped off at the hospital so Dennis wouldn't be alone, while Mark and Kelli went straight to the station. There they told the entire story.

When they'd finished, Kelli said, "And if you don't believe us—" she maneuvered her dress around under the table and pulled the recorder from her new favorite accessory "—pretty sure we recorded the entire thing."

Luckily the police already had believed them. The recording only solidified their next actions. An all points bulletin went out on the missing Hector Mendez. The CEO of the Bowman

Foundation, along with almost all of the staff, were quickly brought in for questioning. Radford Bowman, despite his importance within the foundation, appeared to have no idea what his publicist was up to while on the clock. The lackeys who *had* been working with Hector confirmed Bowman's innocence while condemning those who were not innocent in the least, each trying to swing a deal for their knowledge against Hector.

Mark and Kelli didn't stay long enough to get a head count of how many were in on the scheme. They got the okay to leave with the promise they'd be back the next day.

The sun was coming up by the time Mark and Kelli made it back to his apartment. Nikki greeted them with tight hugs and congratulations for "kicking serious butt." Jonathan had given her the CliffsNotes over the phone and she, too, jokingly offered Kelli a job.

Mark stayed in the living room to fill the

woman in on everything else that had happened while Kelli excused herself to the bedroom. Finally able to take off the dress she had ruined—but knew she'd always keep—Kelli snagged one of Mark's long shirts and unapologetically crawled into his bed.

Grace, feeling the movement, reached for her mother.

Kelli reached right back.

"THIS PLACE IS a dump." To prove his point, Jonathan grabbed the railing and freely wiggled it. The movement nearly took it clear off. Mark rolled his eyes. "I'd never stay here," Jonathan continued.

Mark was with him there. The motel was as run-down as they came. A far cry from what a man like Hector Mendez was probably used to. Yet they had followed him here to the small Florida town's decrepit motel that not even tourists used. It was a perfect place to hide.

If he wasn't being pursued by Orion agents and a private investigator wife. Oliver and Darling Quinn had used every connection in their combined books to follow his trail right to the outside of the one-level motel.

It had been two days since Hector had fled, and Mark was itching to finally take him down. It was a three-way race between Hector fleeing the country, Mark and Orion getting Hector before that, and the FBI agents who had taken over the case catching Hector before anyone else. The Feds had booked it to a town three cities over following up on a reported sighting of the man, along with a credit card used in his name, but Darling had said the information was wrong. She knew more than a few people on the shadier side of the town and was able to track the man to the motel instead. She'd asked if she should let the Feds know of their location but Mark had told her that if and when they caught their man they could give them a ring then.

"Just don't do anything illegal or I'll arrest *you*," the local beat cop, Cara Whitfield, had warned on the ride over. She had talked to the police in Dallas and had been filled in on the possibility that Hector had fled to her small town. It was a possibility she hadn't liked at all. She'd agreed to accompany and help them despite the fact that they weren't truly law enforcement.

Now she stood with the two of them as they stopped to discuss a plan.

"How do you want to play this?" Jonathan asked. Their target was in the room farthest from the office.

"We could always pretend to be housekeeping," Mark offered. "Works for Darling on some of her cases."

"Unless you have a convincing female voice,

I don't think he'll answer the door," Jonathan insisted.

"Hey, men can do housekeeping, too," Mark scolded. "Thinking otherwise is sexist."

Jonathan nodded. "True," he admitted. "Let me say it, then."

Cara made a noise that clearly indicated she was unsure whether or not to be amused.

"Or we can use this," she said, waving a key in the air. "The front-desk clerk said a man fitting Hector's description was the one to pay for the room."

That sobered the men.

"Lead the way," Mark said to the officer. She pulled her gun from her holster.

"Let's try not to get anyone shot."

The three of them sidled to the left of the door. Although Hector was dangerous, the best Cara would let them do was have their stun guns—not cell phone–shaped—as weapons.

That was fine by Mark. He wanted to lay hands on the man. Not bullets.

Despite her annoyance at their antics, Officer Whitfield didn't use the key right off the bat. Instead, she rapped on the door.

"Housekeeping," she called.

No one responded.

"Housekeeping," she tried again.

This time there was a loud crash and scuffling on the other side of the door.

"He's running," Cara yelled, putting the key in the door.

Instead of sticking behind her, Mark turned and ran around the building. He'd already noticed that each room had a back window.

Sure enough, Hector was climbing through it.

"I don't think so," Mark yelled. Hector thumped to the dirt and scrambled to stand.

It didn't work.

Mark threw a punch that put him back on the ground.

Cara was yelling something through the window, but Mark didn't hear it.

"Your luck just ran out, buddy," Mark said.

Hector cradled his jaw, eyes wide in fear. "Let me go and I can make you a very rich man," he said quickly. "You could have everything you've ever dreamed of."

The bodyguard didn't skip a beat.

"Sorry, my dreams can't be bought."

"How about your happiness, then?" Hector whispered angrily as Cara and Jonathan ran up. "You can have *whatever* you want."

Mark pictured Kelli and Grace and smiled.

"What I truly want in life, money can't buy."

Chapter Twenty-Two

Kelli hadn't been in the hospital since she gave birth to Grace. She wasn't afraid of them. She just wasn't comfortable in them. However, she voluntarily walked through the sterile-smelling hallways with determination.

It was time she had a talk with someone.

She finally found the room she was looking for and knocked, oddly nervous. Talking followed by laughter floated out as the door was opened.

Lynn was a little dressier than normal, wearing an orange-and-white floral jumper with matching flats. Her hair was even teased out a bit, with her prettiest hair band secured around her head. It was her smile, though, that was the most beautiful part of her outfit. She was happy, no doubt about it.

Kelli raised her eyebrow at her friend, who promptly averted her gaze.

"Hey, Kel," she greeted her. "Is it time already?"

Kelli smiled. "Yeah, the movers get to the house in an hour," she said. "Everything is all ready to go except Grace's toys and some random knickknacks."

"Where's Mini-You?"

Kelli felt her lips stretch wider. She didn't bother hiding the bigger smile. "She's at the house. She was trying to get Mark to play Pretty Princess with her when I left."

Lynn laughed. "I'll go try to save him," she said, reaching for her purse against the wall. When she straightened, she glanced back in the direction of the hospital bed Kelli couldn't yet see from her spot in the doorway. "Do you want me to stay for this or…?"

"You can leave," Kelli assured her. "I'll be fine."

"Oh, I wasn't worried about you," Lynn shot back with a wink. "I've seen with my own eyes you can handle your own."

They said goodbye, and Lynn left after a few words to the patient over her shoulder. Kelli took a deep breath and went farther into the room.

Dennis Crawford was propped up in bed, hooked up to machines, but also looking a thousand times better than he had when he'd been brought in. One emergency surgery and lots of bed rest had done the man wonders. She even rethought her earlier assumption that he was forty.

"I was wondering when you'd come," he said.

"Apparently life didn't pause itself while we were unknowingly taking down a drug-running operation." She shrugged. It made him laugh, but not too long. He seemed to still be uncomfortable with his healing wounds.

Dennis motioned to the chair next to the bed. It was really close and smelled like Lynn's favorite perfume. Kelli made a mental note to ask her about this new relationship she seemed to be starting. But Lynn had been through a lot recently, so she wouldn't tease her too much just yet.

"How are you feeling?" Kelli asked, unsure of how to talk to the man she'd thought was the ultimate evil just two weeks beforehand.

"Sore but alive. I'm told that you refused to leave me in that basement." He gave her a half smile. "Thank you for that."

"I heard I was returning the favor." She shifted in her seat and stopped dancing around what she wanted to ask. "Tell me everything. Lynn offered, but I wanted to hear it from you."

Like her visit, it seemed Dennis was anticipating Kelli's desire to have him explain as much as he knew. He leaned back against his pillow but held her gaze as he spoke.

"In the beginning, I was contacted directly by Bowman's CEO, Radford, to do a spotlight on the foundation," he started. "It seemed like an open-and-shut story, and I truly thought it was. Until the fire." He averted his eyes for a second, pained. It was an emotion he'd masked well in his office when she'd first confronted him. "Radford came to my office the next day to offer his condolences. I told him I still wanted to honor Victor by printing his last story. He thought that was a great idea. He left, and then a few hours later, Hector showed up. He told me Victor had gotten some names wrong in his story. I didn't believe him. Victor was one of my best writers. Very thorough, especially so close to turn-in. Hector also started acting very strange as he tried to convince me otherwise, but I insisted Victor wouldn't have made that mistake."

"What did Hector say to that?" Kelli found herself leaning in a bit.

"He got angry. Stood up and shut my office door. Then he laid it all out for me."

"He told you about running drugs? Just like that?"

Dennis smirked. It wasn't in humor.

"He was proud of what he'd done. I think he wanted someone who knew what it was like to be successful to be in awe of the success *he'd* achieved." Kelli realized she wasn't that surprised. She could picture Hector's arrogance with ease. "And, in all honesty, I was impressed in a strictly objective way. Turning half of a charity into a cover for running drugs in direct competition with the cartel? That takes serious guts and absolutely thorough planning."

"And a good dose of stupidity," she added.

If the cartel had found out they had lost business because of Hector, he—and everyone connected to him—would have met a very bad end.

"That, too. When he realized that Victor had actually snagged the names of two ex-cartel runners who helped make his venture possible, he panicked. Especially when the calls to the house didn't so much as make Victor think twice. To say Hector escalated quickly is an understatement." He frowned.

"Did he admit he hired Craig to start the fire?"

Dennis nodded. "Those weren't his exact words, but he heavily implied it. He told me he was a well-connected man who wouldn't hesitate in burning me...like Victor had burned." Kelli's jaw tightened. She fisted her hands on her lap. Dennis paused, then continued, voice low. "However, now I know that he wasn't actually all that well-connected. There are very few people who would directly run against the cartel, in direct opposition. And, if he had been so well-connected, I have no doubt that all of us would have met our ends some time ago. Instead, Hector personally visited me and talked to me about covering up the article that could put him in the spotlight. I think his venture was a start-up of sorts and too new for him to really have any allies yet, aside from the lackeys beneath him. Either way, when he came here he must not have believed me when I said I'd keep my mouth shut and change the story—which was good, because I wouldn't have—so he gave me a new incentive."

"Grace," Kelli whispered. After the fire, the secret of her pregnancy had become public.

"And you." His expression softened. "In my line of work, I've had to become a lot of things—hardened, blunt, often seemingly without an ounce of empathy—but something in me seemed to soften, to almost break. What if I did report the real story and wasn't able to get the evidence to put Hector and the whole business away? What if the FBI swooped in and still couldn't manage to get anything to send Hector away for life? I didn't even have Victor's original notes and didn't even know they existed at the time. Every way I looked at it I realized that, for once, I couldn't take a chance on everything falling through. I couldn't gamble with your lives. I wouldn't. So I changed the names the way Hector wanted and hoped you'd never look into it." He gave her a wry smile. "But then you showed up with Victor's original notes and an unwavering amount of loyalty."

That relaxed her a bit. She gave him an apologetic look. "Sorry," she said, not at all meaning it. Dennis waved his hand to dismiss what he also knew was a lie. "How did they know I had the journal?"

Dennis didn't hold back his anger for the answer. "When I came to speak to you at your new house—to try and get you to stop—I had already been visited by Hector. He said if I didn't get you to stop and get the notebook, then you'd pay. He also let me in on the fact that apparently my house was bugged so he could ensure I wasn't up to anything. Something I had suspected but hadn't been able to prove yet. He may have been arrogant but he was also clever."

"So at the Foundation dinner—" she started.

"I gave him the notebook and told him to leave you all the hell alone." He motioned to the fading bruise across his nose. "He wasn't happy."

"I'm sorry," Kelli said, meaning it that time.

"In the end, it turned out better than I could ever have hoped. I heard Mark was able to be the one who grabbed Hector from Florida, right?"

Kelli loved being able to nod at that.

"Mark and Jonathan tracked him down and now the FBI have him back in town. I've since been assured that no amount of money will keep him out of a lifelong prison sentence. I also learned that, thanks to some publication that has been blasting the story all over the internet, the Feds publically confirmed that Hector's entire operation has been shut down while all of those that followed him have admitted to their part in everything. I also couldn't help but notice that my name and Grace's were never mentioned. I think the publication is called the *Scale*?" She smiled and cocked her head to the side. "You wouldn't happen to know anything about that, would you?"

It was Dennis's turn to lie. He shook his head. "I've been attached to this bed since they brought me in. I wouldn't even be able to do that."

Kelli laughed, and just like that, the weight of the unknown lifted. She finally had the entire story behind Victor's death. Justice had been brought not only to the man at the top of the operation but also to those who had helped build his tower.

"Thank you, Dennis," she said, holding his gaze with a look of absolute sincerity. "If Victor were here he would thank you, too." She took his hand in hers and squeezed it.

He squeezed back. "He was a good man."

"Yes, he was."

KELLI PULLED UP to the house for the last time and got out with a much lighter heart. The Dallas weather had been kind enough to revert to its normal heat instead of the freak storms that had plagued the city the past two weeks. If Mark hadn't resigned from his construction job to become a full-time Orion agent again, he probably wouldn't have had work for a while. Kelli couldn't help but smile when she thought about the bodyguard.

After he and Kelli had gotten back from the police station, he'd told Nikki she could go home. He had—with permission—fallen asleep next to Grace and Kelli. Kelli had awoken hours later to the sound of Mark and Grace playing blocks in the living room. Since then, the three of them had fallen into a groove of being together.

One that just felt right.

One that, without saying it aloud, they'd both decided to continue to explore.

One that Kelli hadn't expected but absolutely loved.

"Hello?" she called into the boxed-up house.

"Back here, and please bring your camera," Lynn called.

Kelli, not one to question Lynn's excited voice, pulled her phone out and hurried to Grace's bedroom. Once there, she almost doubled over in laughter.

Mark sat on the floor, a bright pink boa

wrapped around his shoulders, a plastic crown on his head, cheeks tinted with blush. He had a plastic teacup in his hand while Grace—also wearing a crown and blush—sat in Lynn's lap across from him.

"I see someone just had his first taste of Pretty Princess," Kelli said around her fits of laughter. She quickly snapped a picture while she spoke. She looked at Lynn. "I thought you were supposed to help save him?"

Lynn put her hands up in defense. "I tried!"

Mark snorted. "By *tried* she means she tried to get me to wear some of your lipstick," he said. Kelli almost hooted at that.

"Hey, listen here, buddy, I was trying to off-set the blush we had to put on to match your boa," Lynn shot back.

Grace just giggled between them.

"Is this my life now?" Kelli joked.

Mark's lips stretched into a grin. "One can hope," he said.

His words made Kelli's stomach flutter.

Lynn stood and picked up Grace. "Okay, gag me, guys," she said. "You're all over here making Pretty Princess somehow *romantic*. I think it's time we go outside and look for bugs or something, don't you, Grace?"

Grace nodded so hard that her crown nearly fell off. Kelli adjusted it and kissed her forehead before the two left the room.

"Do you want to keep that on or take that off before the movers get here?" Kelli asked the bodyguard.

He shrugged. "I don't know. I think it's a really good color on me," he joked.

"Well, how about I make you a deal?" She walked over to him and took the boa from his neck, her hand lingering beside his cheek. "Help me box the rest of this, and Grace's toys, and I'll let you play dress-up with us whenever you want."

Mark laughed. "Deal."

Together they finished boxing the last of the house's stray contents. Kelli spent the time telling him what Dennis had said. He also admitted his opinion of Dennis had gone up exponentially.

"Lynn's been spending a lot of time at the hospital with him, I've noticed," he added when they had finished.

Kelli put her hands to her ears.

"Yeah, yeah, don't get me started on how weird that is," she said. "But after today's talk, maybe I can come to terms with the possibility of them spending more time together. Then again, when have I ever been able to stop Lynn from dating a man she likes?" She paused, then elaborated, because Mark probably didn't know that answer. "Never."

They conducted a walk-through to make sure everything was ready for the movers. When Kelli was able to confirm that it was, they found themselves standing near the front door in a house devoid of sound. Mark took her hand in his and pulled her close.

Bending down a fraction, he met her lips with a kiss that took her breath away. It put fire in her body and passion back into her heart. He pulled away too soon, much to her disappointment.

"How about I make us all some dinner tonight?" he asked, voice transitioning from husky to an attempt at a normal tone. "I make a mean mac and cheese I'm pretty sure Grace will like better than yours."

Kelli tossed her head back and let the laughter come from her gut.

"I'll believe that when I taste it!"

"Then it's a date," he said, all smiles.

"It's a date."

Mark kissed her forehead and let go of her hand.

"I'll give you a moment," he said without even asking if she needed one.

He already knew she did.

Kelli watched him walk away until the front door closed behind him. She let a moment go by before slipping off her shoes. The hardwood kept her feet cool as she started one truly last walk-through.

The hallway Grace had learned to walk in. The one Victor had carried Kelli through after coming home from their wedding.

The master bedroom where Grace often slept with Kelli when she was afraid of being alone. The same room where Victor had held Kelli until they'd both fallen asleep countless times.

The bathroom with the tub that Grace had dubbed "the rubber duckies' home" with its awful green walls that Victor had promised he'd paint "one of these days."

The spare bedroom that had become Grace's haven. The room that had been waiting for Victor and Kelli's future child.

The kitchen that Grace always ran through,

unaware of her mother's worry of falling. Where once upon a time Victor had tried to convince Kelli his burned lasagna was, in fact, edible.

The living room where all three Cranes had lived, laughed, and loved together and separately.

Kelli paused in the opening of the nook attached to the heart of the home.

The office that had been solely Victor's. She imagined the man at his desk, bent over his laptop with a look of pure concentration on his handsome face.

Kelli couldn't help but smile.

"I love you," she whispered to the quiet.

The urge to say goodbye to the house—to him—faded as she made her way to the living room window. Outside Lynn was doubled over laughing while Grace chased Mark around the yard. He slowed down just enough to let her catch him before turning around to tickle the toddler. She couldn't hear the girl's laughter, but she felt it in her heart.

She would never stop loving Victor—or their only home—and the life they'd had together, but now it was time to be somewhere else.

As if on cue, Mark turned toward the window. His expression softened, and his smile was genuine. Like her daughter's laughter, she felt it in her heart.

One last time, Kelli tried to memorize the cool hardwood against her feet before slipping her shoes back on. She patted the front door and opened it wide.

They would never forget the past, but it was time to start moving toward the future.

As Kelli shut the door behind her and walked toward the laughter of her diverse little family, she knew it was exactly what Victor would have wanted.

* * * * *

MILLS & BOON®

Why shop at millsandboon.co.uk?

Each year, thousands of romance readers find their perfect read at millsandboon.co.uk. That's because we're passionate about bringing you the very best romantic fiction. Here are some of the advantages of shopping at www.millsandboon.co.uk:

* **Get new books first**—you'll be able to buy your favourite books one month before they hit the shops

* **Get exclusive discounts**—you'll also be able to buy our specially created monthly collections, with up to 50% off the RRP

* **Find your favourite authors**—latest news, interviews and new releases for all your favourite authors and series on our website, plus ideas for what to try next

* **Join in**—once you've bought your favourite books, don't forget to register with us to rate, review and join in the discussions

Visit **www.millsandboon.co.uk**
for all this and more today!